A Deadly Di$$olution

Book 8 in By the Numbers series
Featuring Carly Turnquist, forensic accountant

By Leeann Betts

ISBN: 978-1-943688-48-7
(c) 2018

Published by PLS Bookworks, Denver, Colorado
Cover design by Donna Schlachter

Where Publishing Dreams Become Reality

Other Books By Leeann Betts:
Counting the Days: a 31-day devotional
In Search of Christmas Past – a novel
Available at Amazon.com in print & digital, & at Smashwords.com in digital

By the Numbers series featuring Carly Turnquist, forensic accountant
No Accounting for Murder
There Was a Crooked Man
Unbalanced
Five and Twenty Blackbirds
Broke, Busted, and Disgusted
Hidden Assets
Petty Cash
Available at Amazon.com in print & digital, & at Smashwords.com in digital

By Leeann and Donna:
Nuggets of Writing Gold — articles and essays on writing.
More Nuggets of Writing Gold – more articles & essays on writing
Available at Amazon.com in print & digital, & at Smashwords.com in digital

Books by Donna Schlachter:
Second Chances and Second Cups; A short story collection.
The Physics of Love: where the past, the present, and the future collide
The Mystery of Christmas Inn, Colorado
Christmas Under the Stars
Transformation – a devotional

Mended by God series
Broken Dreams, Mended Heart
Broken Dreams, Mended Family
Broken Dreams, Mended Marriage
Available at Amazon.com in print & digital, & at Smashwords.com in digital

From Barbour Publishing:
Echoes of the Heart — The Pony Express Romance Collection
A Prickly Affair — Bouquet of Brides Romance Collection
Train Ride to Heartbreak — Mail Order Brides Romance Collection
Detours of the Heart – MISSadventure Brides (releasing December 2018)

Follow us:
Donna: www.HiStoryThruTheAges.wordpress.com
Leeann: www.AllBettsAreOff.wordpress.com
We are also active on Facebook and Twitter
Sign up for our free quarterly newsletter and receive a free book:
Donna (historical) www.HiStoryThruTheAges.com
Leeann (contemporary) www.LeeannBetts.com

Most people think accountants
live boring lives.

Carly Turnquist is about to
prove them wrong.

They need not account for the money entrusted to them,
because they are acting faithfully.
(II Kings 22:7 NIV)

Bear Cove, Maine, is caught in the 1880's,
its heyday, right where it wants to be.

Carly Turnquist is caught in 2004,
where her story continues.

Tuesday, October 26th

Chapter 1

10:00 a.m.

Carly Turnquist, forensic accountant, inhaled the sweet autumn wind blowing in the window from her garden, wishing she was outside enjoying what might be the last fine day for the season. Living in a small town on the East Coast brought more changeable weather than most people thought possible.

The siren call of the flashing light on her landline overrode whatever wishing or hoping—or even praying—she might do.

Not that she was much of a pray-er.

She sighed and picked up the handset, punched in the code, and listened to the voice message, then disconnected.

No sunny hour in the garden for her.

Work beckoned.

She glanced at her typical office garb: jeans, a sweatshirt, sneakers. It would do.

A command appearance by the mayor wasn't exactly like a summons to tea with royalty.

And his message did say as soon as possible.

She grabbed a pen and notebook, gave Doc, the cat, a quick pat on the noggin, then was on her way. The five-minute trek to Mayor Akerman's office and the return trip would have to count as both her exercise and her outdoor time today.

Under other circumstances, she might have deferred the visit, but there was something in the man's voice that overrode her desire to stay put. Instead, the ember of curiosity that her husband Mike said blazed permanently beneath the surface was stoked into a small bonfire.

She loved a good mystery.

And Walter Akerman's message formed the biggest mystery of her day. And her first job offer from the town of Bear Cove. Maybe this was a way to get her foot—and her nose—in the door and prove her worth as both an accountant and a conscientious resident.

Not to mention, the idea that somebody might be stealing from the town riled her up. Ruffled her feathers, so to speak.

It simply wasn't right.

When she rounded the corner onto Main Street, the crisp breeze off the harbor, bearing the familiar scents of salt water and seaweed, slapped her cheeks and churned her hair. She glanced in the window of the library and sighed. She should have worn a hat. Or tied her unruly shoulder-length locks back. Between the wind and the humidity, she looked like an advertisement for a bad hair day shampoo.

Carly crossed the street and headed for town hall. The green and burgundy awnings contrasted nicely with the pale grey clapboard and green trim.

Up the half dozen steps and in through the double oak doors, then she stopped in her tracks. The former mayor, Wells, who died two years prior in a car accident that was really murder, usually treated this building like he owned it.

But the new mayor, Akerman—finally elected after three false starts in contested elections—seemed intent on removing every hint of personality and history. An abstract metal piece that might have been fashioned by third graders occupied the focal point of the entryway, where a statue of Jacob Roy's grandfather once stood. Greenery reminiscent of Christmas garland replaced the faded bunting from President Roosevelt's tour of the area in the early 1940's, which once hung from the railing of the second floor.

She shrugged. Personally, she liked the old stuff. The nicked edges and waning colors felt familiar, like old friends. This new stuff? Cold. A reminder that few things stay the same.

Carly disliked change. She often said she didn't have a problem with change so long as she wasn't there when it happened.

Well, they didn't ask her opinion about these minor renovations. And a good thing.

She'd say save the money and leave it. It was good enough for the past seventy years, it'd be good enough for the next seventy.

Probably her frugal mid-western upbringing. Or her accountant's nose to improve the bottom line.

Or the fact she didn't like these particular changes.

She sighed. Change. Inevitable. But it didn't mean she couldn't resist it.

She strolled the hallway leading to the mayor's office, once again noting the aged and faded portraits of former heads of the town. From muttonchops and morning jackets in the 1880's, to tweed blazers through most of the previous century, until finally she stood eye to eye with Mayor Wells. A smidge of an ache at his senseless death formed, then she moved on to Walter Akerman's likeness— this one an active and updated rendition of the traditional photo— Akerman on the golf course.

Her brow pulled down. If he wanted to promote the idea of being community minded and available, this image might do the trick. Except Bear Cove had no golf course, so apparently his accessibility was limited to other venues. Not to mention, some—like her—might wonder when he got his mayoring work done—between tee-off times?

He should have chosen a casual stance like sitting on the corner of his desk, arms folded, shirt collar unbuttoned. A semi-full inbox to suggest he was a busy man who got things done. Photos of his family arrayed behind him to indicate strong local connections. Perhaps a few publicity shots of glad-handing with business people from town.

Oh well. Not her job.

She had enough to do without taking on something nobody asked her about.

Probably because most people thought she was a boring fuddy-duddy with her head in a calculator and her pencil in the sharpener.

She chuckled. Those people hadn't checked with Mike lately.

The door to the mayor's office opened, and a woman dressed primly in a long sleeved sweater, pencil-line skirt, and low-heeled pumps exited, files in her arm.

Carly smiled and dipped her head. "Hi, Evie."

A flush ran up the middle-aged secretary's neck and cheeks, complementing her dark hair. "Carly. He's ready. Go right on in."

So unlike Mayor Wells's bulldog-like gatekeeper, Miss Cook, who retired after the unfortunate incidents involving a nudist colony and missing money.

Carly nodded and waved, then entered the office. The room had been repainted and updated in the months since the election, and now boasted a cheery shade of buttery yellow on the walls, offset with a brilliant white on the ceiling and trim. A potted plant of daisies picked up the palette, lending a feeling of being in a field on a warm summer's day.

A happy place.

The door leading to Mayor Akerman's office stood open, and she crossed the room, her shoes tapping on the refinished hardwood floors. She caught a glimpse of the mayor, paused and rapped, entering when he waved her in.

Walter Akerman sat behind his desk, papers spread out. Building plans of some sort. He rolled the documents and set them to one side, then stood and offered his hand. "Thanks for coming so quickly, Carly."

She returned the shake. "You caught me at a good time. Just finished a project for a client. And you said it was important."

He gestured to two wingback chairs set around a low coffee table. "Let's sit here. I always feel like I've been called to the principal's office when somebody sits across the desk from me."

She chuckled then sat. Despite her misgivings about his photo in the hallway, she was going to like this man. "Been there, done it."

"I bet you have." He lifted a coffee pot and raised a brow in question, to which she nodded. "Let's settle in for a minute. We haven't had a chance to get to know each other."

"I'd like that." She had nothing better to do right now. She sipped her coffee. Delicious. Better coffee? Or perhaps the china cup and saucer. She'd need to be careful not to break it. Or spill it on herself. "Are you settling in to the job?"

He glanced around the office. "Think so. Sometimes I wonder why I'm not more nervous about the whole thing. Maybe it's because I don't know enough to be worried."

Yes, she was definitely going to like him. "Been there, done it."

"How about you?" He peered at her over the rim of his cup. "You're not a native, are you?"

"No. Moved here when I married Mike almost fifteen years ago. Most people accept that I'm here to stay. Unless if I try to get involved in important things like choosing what color to paint the library. Then I'm shunned like Typhoid Mary."

Folks in Bear Cove were a funny lot. Despite solving multiple murders, saving people's lives, revealing nefarious plots to embezzle or steal, those born and raised in the town still held her at arm's length. Except for a few compassionate souls, like Mrs. Olsen at the pharmacy, or Jacob Roy at the garage.

The mayor set his cup on the table. "Understood. Thankfully I'm at least a third generation native."

"If you weren't, you wouldn't have won the election."

"Right. The last time, I ran against a man related to an original town father. Nobody stood a chance there."

"I've heard good things from folks." That was true. She wouldn't offer up empty flattery—not even to get a town contract. "I think the town needs some peace and quiet. After all that's happened in the last few years."

"Which is why I wanted to use somebody local to look at the town's financial records. If I brought in a big firm from outside, word would be around town in about two minutes."

She pulled out her notebook and pen. "What's the problem?"

"Money is being moved around to various unconnected accounts, including assets and liabilities, from expenses and income. With no obvious reason. No explanation other than a notation about correcting a previous error. A couple of those I can understand, but this is dozens of them."

"Has something changed in the accounting methods used by the town?"

"Such as?"

She glanced up from her notes. "Have you changed your accounting method from cash to accrual? Or vice versa? Or did the fiscal year end change?"

He shook his head. "Nothing like that. We've used the same accounting firm for years. I checked with them. They don't know anything about it. All of the entries happened in the last six months or so."

"Since your election."

"Right."

"And you think?"

"I think somebody is stealing from the town, and trying to make it look like I'm involved."

$ $ $

All the way back to her house, Carly studied every person she saw. Was she the thief? Or perhaps him? The school crossing guard? The bank teller?

Surely not somebody she knew.

Then again, she knew just about everybody. In a town boasting four hundred souls at the height of lobster season, there weren't many unfamiliar faces. And most of them were likely tourists or folks visiting residents.

No, most likely, she knew the perpetrator.

As she walked up to her front door, her mind raced with the mayor's revelation. How a quiet, east coast town like Bear Cove ended up with so many criminals was beyond her.

A perfunctory look at the town's financial records confirmed the mayor's suspicion: someone was doctoring the books and trying to cover their trail.

Who, she didn't know. Yet.

She inserted the key into the lock and stepped inside. The landline rang.

She dropped the bag of files and stepped over Doc to answer it. "Hello?"

"Carly, it's Sarah."

Her daughter-in-love, a young woman Carly loved like her own daughter. Married for just over a year. Wife to Mike's son Tom from his previous marriage. Adoptive parents of Mike and Carly's nephew Bradley following his father's passing.

"Hey, Sarah. What's up?"

"Tom and I have to go to LA for work, and Bradley was wondering if he could come stay a few nights. Because of the lunar eclipse. His school says any kids who want to take a couple of days off to watch it up close and personal and agree to write a report about their experience can do so. And Friday is an in-service for teachers. We get back late Friday night and could drive down on Saturday and get him."

Carly smacked her forehead. She completely forgot about the eclipse. "Sure. Will you drive him?"

"Not a chance. He wants to take the bus. Is that okay? I can get him on one that arrives just before supper today if that works for you."

"That would be fine. Mike is out of town for today, but he'll be back this evening. I think we can find something to entertain ourselves until then. You two lovebirds enjoy a couple of romantic evenings to yourselves."

Sarah chuckled. "Right. Work with clients all day and stay up half the night revising to show them what they want the next day. We'll be lucky to do anything more than room service."

"Hopefully you'll get at least one dinner out at a nice restaurant."

"Maybe Friday evening. To celebrate. If we can squeeze it in before the flight. Maybe at the airport."

Carly chuckled. "Oh, yeah, that's romantic. MickeyD's all around."

She said her goodbyes then hung up, remaining slouched on the sofa. Thinking about her kids, as she called them—Mike's son and daughter, really, but hers in her heart—reminded her of their week together a couple of months ago on Cape Cod. That was seven days jam-packed with adventure. Losing Toby on the way. A body. A mysterious friend for the kids. The kids missing. Counterfeit money.

And so much talk about faith and God.

She still wasn't sure where she stood with all that, but one thing was for sure: Denise and her husband Don exhibited a peace in the midst of all that turmoil she wished she had.

And if it came from faith—well, she'd check it out. When she had time.

Right now, she had a room to get ready for an active little boy.

And dinner to plan and prepare.

A house to tidy.

And about a hundred pounds of paper records to sift through and organize.

She had her work cut out for her.

$ $ $

Carly glanced at the clock on her computer. Why did she always think she had plenty of time, then spend her last precious moments dashing around like a madwoman?

Probably because—as her father used to say—everything takes more time and more money than she thought.

He was right again.

Preparing the bedroom for her nephew's—now her grandson's—she never quite knew which term to use—stay took more than the ten minutes she allotted because it hadn't been deep-cleaned in months. And as much as she hated cleaning, she wouldn't let him sleep in a room with cobwebs and dust bunnies big enough to attack and overtake Doc. Laundry, vacuuming, dusting, sorting through the dresser drawers to clear out a couple so he could unpack and feel at home then going through the closet to make room for his hanging clothes. . .

Three hours later, she'd paused to take a shower and change her outfit before popping a roast into the oven and setting the table.

And then to work.

Now, another three hours later, she had about five minutes to make it to the bus depot on time. If there was one thing she hated, it was coming home and not have somebody right there to meet her. After all, if it was important that she visit, it should be important enough to her hosts to be there ahead of time.

She tossed her pen on the desk and set the papers aside, then slipped her feet into her plimsoles, grabbed her keys, and headed out the door and into her car.

Four minutes.

Bear Cove's definition of rush hour—three pickups, a tractor, and a hay wagon—crept along Main Street. She peered out her open window, trying to see around the cloud of exhaust and wide vehicles ahead of her.

Three minutes.

She could have walked there faster. She gritted her teeth and clenched the steering wheel. Maybe the bus was late.

Two minutes.

A couple of middle-aged tourists—judging by their sparkly visors and capris pants—jaywalked across in front of the car in front of her.

One minute.

Finally, the tractor and wagon pulled over, and the three pickups surged ahead.

She glanced up the street at the depot as the bus pulled into its parking space.

Time's up.

She yanked the wheel hard and slid to a stop in front of the bus, facing the wrong direction, as the door opened with a swish and the first passengers disembarked.

She jumped out and rounded the front of her sedan as Bradley emerged and looked around.

She waved. "Over here."

He smiled and hoisted a backpack higher on his shoulder then trotted to her, allowing her to pull him into a grandma-sized hug.

She kissed the top of his head—goodness, he'd grown since she saw him in August—and turned his face toward her. "You are more handsome every time I see you. And taller, too."

He puffed out his chest as though both attributes were as a result of his hard work. "I've been arm wrestling with Dad, and I even beat him sometimes."

Dad.

Surely the sweetest words a man could hear.

Bradley had worked his way into her children's home and their hearts.

She turned toward the car. "Is that all you have?"

"Nope. Got my telescope, and my camera, and my night lens."

She stopped and turned back toward the bus. "Goodness. Sounds like you plan on staying a while."

He turned solemn eyes to her. "Just four nights. Is that okay? Maybe Grampa Mike could take me fishing again."

She tousled his hair. "Maybe he could."

"Hey, lady, turn this way."

Carly turned at the words, and a man in olive-green cargo pants, a rumpled shirt, brown sneakers, and a backwards ball cap snapped her picture.

Who was this man? And why was he taking her picture?

$ $ $

As the older woman with the kid strode toward him, Harvey Paulson took a step back.

She didn't look the friendly type he always associated with small towns.

Then again, maybe he aroused a she-bear protectiveness, what with the kid there and all.

He doffed his cap then replaced it, covering his four-month-old haircut—and his bald spot. Too old for implants, not too old to be self-conscious, regardless of the quips about extra testosterone and handsome baldies. "Ma'am. Good day."

She planted fists on her hips. Well, at least they weren't aimed at his nose.

"Who are you and why are you taking our picture?"

"Harvey Paulson. Journalist in town to cover the eclipse. Thought I'd start with some human interest stuff. You know, about how nice the folks of Bean Cove are."

He pulled a business card from one of the cargo pockets in his pants and handed it toward her, never releasing it. No point anybody having evidence that maybe he fudged the truth a tad.

She read it then nodded. "First of all, it's *Bear* Cove. You'd best not mispronounce it again or somebody is likely to toss you into the harbor."

Good advice. Nothing like a swim in the ocean in October to instill a lesson. He should know. He'd been there once or twice before. He tucked the card back into his shirt pocket. "I'll keep that in mind."

"And secondly, I think you need a release to print our photos."

"Not if I don't show your face."

She tipped her head to one side as she considered this information. "Really?"

"So long as you're not recognizable."

She snorted. "Well, you won't be able to publish it without my release. Everybody knows me in town. And they know my grandson."

"Doesn't matter. But if it makes you happy, I won't publish your picture."

"All right then."

Good, that seemed to take the wind out of her sails.

The kid spoke up. "Mister, are you really a reporter?"

Harvey straightened his shoulders. "They call us journalists now. But yeah, I'm a reporter. And a photographer. I write the story, take the pictures, the whole shebang."

"And you're here to cover the eclipse?"

"That's what I said, kid."

"Me, too."

Might be fun to play along with him. "I'd better watch out for the competition, then, huh? You might get a big scoop."

The boy's forehead wrinkled. "Scoop?"

"Yeah, that's when one journalist has the inside information on a big story and gets his paper to publish it before another one. It's called a scoop."

"I'm not here for a scoop. I'm here to see the eclipse and write a report for school."

"Well, that's kind of what I do. I go around asking questions, taking pictures, and then I write a report."

The kid patted his backpack. "I have a camera, and a telescope. And a notebook and pencil. What else do I need?"

Harv tapped his temple. "An inquiring mind." He looked to the woman. "Okay if we talk a minute?"

She relaxed about a millimeter and nodded. "I guess so."

He pulled a pen and paper from his shirt pocket. "You know my name. Care to share yours?"

"Carly Turnquist." When he scribbled her name, she held up a hand. "But I don't want to see either my name or my picture in the paper. Agreed?"

"Come on, Carly. I'm just trying to do my job. I think a special interest piece on our young journalists and scientists would be just the thing to put this berg on the map."

"Bear Cove is already on the map."

"Yes, a very tiny dot in a small state."

Her brow furrowed. "The eclipse is already giving us more publicity than we want."

"What are you? The Chamber of Commerce? And what town doesn't want people to visit? Besides Hotel California, I mean."

She tipped her head in question.

"You know. You can go in but you can't get out?" What bubble did she live in? "Never mind." He turned to the kid. "What's your name, son?"

"Bradley Turnquist."

Harvey scratched the name on his notepad. "She your mother?"

The woman laid a protective hand on the boy's shoulder. "Nice try, but no. I'm his grandmother. And his picture and name are not to be used, either. He's a minor."

"Lady, lady. I'm not the boogieman here. Just trying to do my job. I'm here to cover the eclipse—"

"Which doesn't happen until tomorrow night. Good day."

"You're killing me, lady. Well, if another paper gets the scoop on me, it'll be on your head."

The boy hung back, resisting her firm hand on his arm. "What happens if somebody else gets the scoop before you, Mr. Paulson?"

"I'll just die if that happens. Just die."

Chapter 2

5:30 p.m.

Carly glanced over at Bradley as they rode back to the house. The vehicles ahead crept along like molasses uphill in December. "So, what do you want to do for the rest of the day?"

"Thought I'd set up my telescope in your back yard and practice focusing on things. And I want to take some pictures tonight. Make sure I have the right settings."

"Sounds complicated."

"It's not, if you know what you're doing."

She chuckled. "You've been listening to your dad. Or your Grampa Mike."

"Both." The boy fiddled with the knob on the radio. "Don't you have any good stations out here?"

"Out here?" She smiled in his direction. "You make it sound like we live out in the boonies."

"Almost."

She mock-punched his arm. "You keep that up, and I just might send you to the real boonies. They make Bear Cove look positively continental."

"Seriously, Gramma Carly. You only have one station?"

"Can only listen to one at a time."

"Now you've been listening to Dad."

"Where do you think he learned it?"

Bradley settled back into his seat and stared out the window.

"Why is there so much traffic?"

"Not sure." She drifted over the center line to get a better view of the vehicles ahead. "I was wondering the same thing."

The van in front of them stopped, so Carly eased to a halt.

Right across the street from the Dew Drop Inn, an empty parking spot. As if put there for their benefit.

She pulled her sedan in and parked. "I think it's time for something to eat. It must be supper time, and Grampa Mike won't be home until later. I've got a roast in the oven, but it'll switch off on its own. And we can have sandwiches tomorrow. What do you think?"

Bradley made a big show of checking his watch, an oversized black rubber thing with every timepiece bell and whistle she'd ever seen. And some she hadn't. "Let's see."

She opened her door. "I don't care what time it is. Or what you think. I'm going to the café. Coming with?"

He hesitated about two milliseconds before nodding. "Bus travel can make a man hungry."

She smiled at his referring to himself as a man. All of nine years old, and mature beyond his years. Most likely because of the life he and his birth father, Jerry, lived.

She shivered. Although losing his dad was traumatic, the dark cloud was turned inside out. Immediate fostering and adoption by Tom and Sarah meant a stability the boy never knew before.

Not to mention, no abuse.

While at first she resented Mike's brother's intrusion in their lives—the mysteries, the lies, and the stealing—the outcome was Bradley, now her grandson instead of only being her nephew.

What a tangled family tree.

She gripped his hand, although at first he tried to wrestle his fingers from her, and they trotted across the street. Carly waved to Chief Donovan when he slowed his patrol car to give them the right of way, tossing him a mock grimace. She was jaywalking. And encouraging a child to do the same.

He waved her on then accelerated toward the bus station.

He probably didn't like the increased traffic any more than she did.

In fact, if Bear Cove had its way, it would post a sign on the highway saying, NO SERVICES. DON'T COME HERE.

Not that the town really needed a sign. Most of the residents were of that mindset, and few people visited before deciding to move here permanently. She lived here for more than fifteen years, and she still wasn't considered a *real* native.

She pushed through the wooden door of the diner and paused to inhale the scents of fried onions, strong coffee, and doughnuts. All of the tables were occupied, but two stools at the counter beckoned. She headed in that direction with Bradley so close behind, his toes nipped at her ankles. Thankfully she didn't have far to go.

Carly slid into a chair with a chrome back and cracked vinyl seat repaired with electrical tape.

In a booth behind her, Molly, the receptionist from the radio station, called out. "Hi, Carly. Does your husband know you're having dinner with a handsome younger man?"

Bradley's cheeks colored, and Carly chuckled and patted him on the back. "I hope you never lose the good grace to blush at a compliment."

"Doesn't she know who I am?"

"Of course she does. She's just teasing."

He buried his face in a menu. "I don't like to be teased."

Carly rubbed his back a moment, and his shoulders relaxed. "It's how people show you they like you."

He looked up at her. "Could you ask her not to like me so much?"

"If I do, she'll probably do it even more. If it really bothers you, the best thing is to ignore her. She'll stop if she doesn't see you react."

He straightened his shoulders. "Okay. I'll try."

"Good boy." Carly scanned the single-page food choices. "Let's see. What will we have?"

"Cheeseburger and fries. And a soda."

"Sounds good."

The only waitress in the place, Victoria, approached. Middle-aged, her hair pulled back into a bun and covered with a hairnet, smiled and tapped a pencil on her order pad. "What can I get for you?" She peered over her bifocals perched on the tip of her nose. "Bradley, right? Good to see you again, son. Been a while."

"Yes, ma'am."

Her eyes widened. "I declare you've grown a foot since I last saw you."

"No, ma'am, just about four inches. But it's been a while."

Victoria smiled at him then turned to Carly. "He's sure polite. Not like those that go around with their ball caps on backwards and their pants hanging down to their knees." She pointed to the menu before Bradley. "Everything on there is good. What do you want?"

They placed their orders and settled back to wait. Victoria set their sodas in front of them then bustled away to another customer at the far end of the counter. Carly sipped the cold drink and studied the other patrons using the mirror over the counter. Molly shared her booth with another woman Carly didn't recognize. Mrs. Bailes, the librarian, waved to her, and Carly returned the gesture. The woman was most helpful in filling Carly in on the goings-on in the town council when that new company wanted to renovate the MacQuarrie estate just outside town.

Apart from them, the rest of the booths were filled with men and women she didn't recognize, which was unusual for a Tuesday in October in Bear Cove. Probably also explained the lack of parking in front of the diner.

She focused on three men and a woman who occupied the booth behind her and to her left. They appeared to know each other as they laughed and talked, but they didn't look to be close friends or relatives. Co-workers, she guessed. No one person led the conversation, and they didn't defer to one over the other.

And, when the bill came, they each fished money from wallets and tossed it on the table.

Equals.

But at what?

When Victoria placed their plates heaped with a gigantic burger and enough fries to choke a horse in front of them, Carly's curiosity burst forth. She quirked her head in the direction of the foursome. "Who are they?"

Victoria's mouth turned down. "Some kind of reporters." She quirked her chin toward Carly's plate. "Soggy fries, just the way you like 'em."

"For what?" Carly popped a fry into her mouth and savored the salty, oily sogginess for what it was—ambrosia. "You planning to kill somebody and make the ten o'clock news?"

Victoria frowned at her. "You're a fine one to talk about murder, Miss Sherlock Holmes."

Bradley giggled, and Carly silenced him with The Look. "It's not like I look for mysteries. Or bodies."

"No, you're just a magnet for them." Victoria's expression eased. "They're covering the eclipse."

"Who knew a natural phenomenon could generate so much interest?"

"Seems the rest of the eastern seaboard west to the Mississippi is forecasting cloud cover. Bear Cove just became the prime spot to see the eclipse."

"Wow, Gramma, that's great. The other kids won't have good reports to give. I should get a good grade."

Carly patted the boy's arm. "You'll get a good mark if you write a good report. The grade should be based on the report, not on how much you could see. Those other kids have no control of the weather. Would you like it if it was the other way around, and you came here and it was cloudy?"

His smile fell away. "Guess not."

Victoria nodded. "Your grandmother's right, Bradley. We should never gloat over another's misfortune. That's what the Good Book says, too."

Carly added mustard to her burger and decided to ignore the waitress's reference. "How many reporters are in town?"

Victoria shrugged. "Not sure. Been about twenty of them in here already today. And the eclipse doesn't happen until tomorrow night, so I expect more will come will show up. 'Specially with the weather forecast."

"Where will they all stay? Bear Cove is about as hospitable as a porcupine. The closest motel is up on the highway to Riverdale."

The waitress leaned in close. "I hear some people are making out gangbusters on this little windfall. They're renting out their spare rooms, their attics, their yards to park motor homes. Even leaving town and renting out their entire house." She straightened. "I hear what as some are getting a hundred dollars a night." She tsk-tsked with her tongue. "I don't know what this town is coming to."

Maybe into the twentieth century? Finally.

Carly shrugged. "I guess they figure if people are going to come anyway, they might as well make a few dollars."

"You don't think it's wrong?"

"Not particularly. How are the reporters finding out who's got a room?"

"Word of mouth."

Carly picked up her burger. "Well, then, that's all right. It's not like they're advertising."

The older woman nodded. "Maybe I could rent out my spare room. Seems a shame for one of them to have to drive all the way to Riverdale for a place to lay their head."

Her burger called to her, but eating and talking at the same time wasn't a skill Carly had mastered. She always managed to spit crumbs, or choke on something, or end up with mustard on her clothes. Best to get Victoria back to doing what she did best—waiting on tables.

She nodded. "You might drop a hint that if they need lodging, you have a room."

Victoria's smile returned. "Good idea. And if anybody asks, I'll tell them you suggested that to me."

Carly groaned inwardly as Victoria left. Great. Another black mark against her in the eyes of some of the townspeople. Encouraging strangers to stay.

She sank her teeth into the squishy bun, the cool lettuce and tomato, and the hot meat. Now *this* was ambrosia times four. As she chewed, she checked out the street in the mirror. Three vans emblazoned with logos from television stations north and south of town inched past, heading into town. Two more worked their way in the other direction. Five stations represented. Who knew there were that many?

Mrs. Bailes and her dining companion rose to leave, pausing at the counter a moment. "Carly, I'd like to introduce you to Anita Blake. She's on the town council, and she works at the hospital as a nurse."

Carly wiped her hands in a napkin before shaking with Anita. "Nice to meet you. Don't know how we've managed not to bump into each other before."

The woman reminded her a little of her former friend Susan with her professionally manicured nails and designer suit. Carly glanced at her own hands. Stained by mustard, greasy from the fries, in desperate need of lotion.

Anita's lopsided smile—an affliction or an affectation?—slipped a mite. "How do you do?"

Non-committal. Sounded like a politician. Even in a small town like Bear Cove, where the next election win or loss was a single snub away.

Mrs. Bailes looked from one to the other then pasted on a smile. "Well, great. Nice to see you again, too, Bradley."

His mouth full of burger, Bradley had the good grace to nod and smile in her direction.

Obviously the boy took after his grandfather, and not his grandmother.

Anita turned back to her. "I hear the mayor asked you to look into the town's books. Is there a problem?"

"I'm sure if there is, he'll tell you. Nothing wrong with another set of eyes."

The woman's own gaze narrowed. "Yes, well, just as long as he isn't looking for trouble where none exists."

"I doubt he is."

"Well, I know him a *lot* better than you do, and I think it's safe to say Walter Akerman is always looking for a scapegoat." She lowered her voice. "You might want to duck when he starts flinging mud."

The councilor straightened and strode from the diner, her heels clicking on the linoleum flooring.

Mrs. Bailes raised her eyebrows in question, but Carly had no answer for her. The librarian trotted out behind her.

Bradley set his burger down. "Why would the mayor throw dirt?"

"Huh?"

"She said he flings mud."

"Oh, that's just a figure of speech. It means she thinks he might try to blame things on other people."

His eyes widened. "Even if they didn't do it?"

"I don't know. I guess it's possible."

"Why would someone do that? Isn't that lying?"

"I don't know why, but it is lying. Let's eat our dinner and not worry about it, okay?"

"Okay."

The boy returned to his lunch, attacking the last of the fries with vigor.

But Carly pushed her food around on her plate. Something happened here which seldom occurred.

She suddenly lost her appetite.

$ $ $

Two hours later, Carly pushed papers away from her. No doubt about it—money was missing. Despite a convoluted series of journal entries moving numbers from one general ledger account to another, from one asset type to an expense account, and from bank accounts to investment accounts to income accounts, the net result was about a hundred thousand dollars less in the town's bank accounts than should be.

All of it since Walter Akerman's election.

The other councilors were veterans, including the hoity-toity Anita Blake, who looked like she had as much money as she needed—which was interesting in itself. It was hard to believe her entire excessive-looking lifestyle was funded as a nurse in a town as small as Bear Cove. Was the woman simply civic-minded and doing her part for the town, or had she sought election for access to the town's funds?

Could be some satisfaction if that was why she served on the council.

She left her office and went to the kitchen. Her half-eaten burger and soggy fries beckoned to her, so she popped the takeout container into the microwave. One thing that invigorated her was hunting down assets.

While the appliance hummed doing its thing, she peeked out through the kitchen window. At the far end of the yard, Bradley fiddled with his telescope. Most likely, as soon as Mike pulled in the yard, the two would be out there until midnight, making miniscule adjustments that she wouldn't understand even if she asked.

Which she wouldn't.

Mike didn't understand her methods, and she rarely comprehended his.

What was that saying? A riddle wrapped in a mystery inside an enigma.

That was her husband.

And, it appeared, her grandson, too.

The microwave dinged and she retrieved the now slightly-melted package and headed back to work. She wasn't getting paid to conduct surveillance on her grandson.

Now that she confirmed the mayor's suspicions, he'd need evidence to pass along to Chief Donovan.

Which meant somebody in this town—perhaps somebody she knew well—was a thief.

If her dislike for a person were the only criteria, the criminal would be Anita Blake. But that wasn't evidence.

First she'd start with a list.

And as much as she hated to admit, Ms. Blake wasn't the logical chief suspect.

Mayor Akerman was.

But why the man would hire her to reveal a theft that so far escaped everybody else's notice was beyond her.

But maybe not.

Maybe he wanted her to stop him. Perhaps he was calling out for help. Or he was schizophrenic and the honest side of him didn't know the thief was his dishonest self.

Like Dr. Jekyll and Mr. Hyde.

Probably not.

That made a good story, but in real life? Unlikely.

She sat at her desk, popped open the Styrofoam container, and selected a fry with her left hand while scribbling names on a notepad at her elbow with her other.

Okay. As much as she hated to do it: Mayor Akerman.

But Anita Blake came next.

Who else had access to the town's bank account?

The treasurer, Gail Sullivan. She worked as a manicurist from her home right across the street from the community hospital. Active on a lot of committees. Single. Nothing Carly knew about her or her lifestyle shouted embezzler.

Bob Whalen, the town manager. A paramedic. Married with three boys. His wife, Clarisse, liked to play hostess. Their oldest was in college, the next two, a set of twins, would go next year.

She paused. Three kids in college would be costly. And Clarisse had expensive tastes, judging from the pale pink convertible she drove around town.

But she came from money. Or so Carly heard. And if that was true, unlikely Bob needed to steal.

Maybe Evie Mack had access through her boss to the books, but she doubted it. And Evie just didn't strike her as the type to steal. A little mousey. Preferred ten-year-old classic suits.

What about someone working at the bank? She jotted down Aroostook National Bank. Ever since that episode with the staged robbery and the mess with Jerry, she avoided actually going into the building, choosing to use the ATM and the night deposit. Mike thought she was being silly, but not enough time had passed to ease her suspicions that they still talked about the event, even though she was completely vindicated.

She put a question mark after the bank's name.

That left the accounting firm. But she had no idea who did their annual audit. She made a note to ask the mayor.

That done, she turned her attention to the next item on her list: finish her dinner.

She had no doubt she'd succeed at that task.

$ $ $

Mike parked next to Carly's car in the driveway, glad to be home. And even more glad that his wife was home. He exited and locked his SUV, and headed for the house. Now, for a nice, quiet evening together. Rehash their day. Maybe early to bed. . .

What the—

He tripped over a bag of some kind just inside the foyer, kicking it aside so he could close the door. The coffee table was littered with soda cans and potato chip bags. Every light was on in the house.

Was he in the right place?

Must be—the key worked in the lock. Sure, he heard of cars that could be opened with a key from a different make and model, but never heard that same story about a house. And the car one was probably an urban myth.

So he must be in his own home.

All kinds of crazy scenarios ran through his mind, including burglars who ate snacks, invasion of the body snatchers, and a party he didn't remember not being invited to.

He strolled through the living room and into the kitchen. Doc lounged on his cat castle, peering through the window into the dark back yard.

Strange. Something was sure holding the cat's attention.

Mike peered through the glass in the door. Two figures huddled together at the far end of the yard. Nodding and pointing. Fiddling with something.

He glanced around. His first hunch was right. They'd been burgled. And now the crooks were dividing up their booty before they beat a hasty retreat.

A weapon. He needed to find a weapon.

Wait a minute. They were already out of the house. He could simply lock them out for sure.

He slid the deadbolt into place.

Carly. Where was she? Her car was in the drive. Didn't mean she was home, of course. She could have gone for a walk. No, not his wife. Her preferred form of exercise was jumping to conclusions.

He slipped down the hallway to the office. Not there. Nothing looked disturbed. Bathroom was empty. Bedroom, too. Laundry closet? Nope. Not unless they stuffed her into a dryer.

He didn't think the dimensions were conducive to such an act, but he checked anyway.

So where was she?

Why was every light on?

Who made the mess in the living room?

And speaking of living room, what kind of burglars broke in and didn't take anything except whatever potato chips and soda they could consume?

His heart slowed down a notch. He obviously was spending way too much time with his wife—seeing a mystery around every corner.

A knock at the back door caught his attention.

Burglars don't usually knock.

Still, he snatched up a steak knife on the way to answer it.

He'd show them what-for.

He peered through the glass again.

Carly.

And Bradley.

Feeling more than a little foolish, and glad they weren't there to witness his fruitless house search, he set the knife on the counter and unlocked the door.

Carly hugged him close and planted a kiss on his mouth.

Now that was a homecoming.

And his nephew—no, make that his grandson, Bradley, followed close behind. Mike reached to hug him, and Bradley gave him an awkward one-armed version, his other hand toting some kind of duffle bag thing.

Once he closed the door again, he turned to face them. "What are you guys doing out in the dark?"

Carly's glance rested on the knife, now out of position from its normal knife block next to the stove, and smirked at him. "Did we scare you?"

Mike waved off her words. "Not at all. Force of habit, you know, locking the doors after dark." He tousled the boy's hair. "Didn't know you were coming for a visit."

Carly led the way to the living room and Mike joined her on the sofa while Bradley sat in the wingback chair near the door. "Yeah, Sarah called. He has a few days off school to write a report on the eclipse. Tom and Sarah will pick him up on Saturday."

Mike wrapped an arm around his wife's shoulders. So much for a quiet evening at home. "What's in the duffle bag?"

"My telescope and camera." He pulled out the scope. "I was practicing setting it up. Taking some night photos." He turned to Carly. "Can I get the pictures developed tomorrow?"

She nodded. "Sure. I can take the film up to the place on the highway. They have a one-hour lab."

The boy smiled. "Thanks." He patted a notebook in his shirt pocket. "I keep a record of every picture I take, the settings and the f-stop and exposure, see what works, and repeat."

Mike stacked his feet on the coffee table. "Sounds like a science."

"It is."

Mike clasped his hands behind his head, glad to be home, even though any thoughts of cuddling with his wife flew out the window. For now. "I have time tomorrow if you want help."

Bradley pursed his lips. "Well, we're supposed to do it ourselves. Would it be okay to go down near the park and look for a place that gives a good view of the eastern sky?"

Carly looked to Mike who nodded. "Sure, that's fine. Pretty much everybody around town knows you."

Mike's cell phone vibrated in his pocket. He stood and dug it out. "I need to take this call. Back in a minute."

He headed for the kitchen. This was one secret Carly wouldn't uncover. He worked hard to keep the details from her. "Hi, it's Mike."

"Hi, Mike. Dr. Nick here."

"Thanks for returning my call, Dr. Nick. Is everything set up?"

"Yes. The earliest date I could get is next year."

"Oh, that long."

"I know you were hoping for something sooner, but with all the hoops we gotta jump through with corporate, you know. . . "

"No, I understand. The waiting is the worst. What date?"

"May 25th. It's the Monday of the Memorial Day weekend. Lots of folks listen to the radio while they're in the car or working around the house. She'll have the whole day. But here's the thing. It's the only day I could get the bigwigs to agree to. If that doesn't work, it's a no-go."

"I'll check and then get back to you."

"Sounds good. And thanks for thinking of me. I know our people are looking forward to it."

Mike disconnected. May 25th. It was a while off. Surely they could organize their schedule to take a weekend mini-vacation. That's how he'd couch it to her—let's go to Portland for the weekend. Keep the real purpose a secret as long as he could. No way would she weasel this out of—

"Mike?"

He snapped his phone shut. "I need to get you a bell for around your neck. You shouldn't sneak up on folks like that."

She grinned. "Or I might find myself at the sharp end of a steak knife."

"What did you think I'd do? I come home. You're not here. The place is a mess. I thought we were burgled."

She slid her arms around his waist and laid her head on his chest.

"That's so sweet." She looked up at him. "Who was that?"

"Nobody."

"I heard you mention a doctor."

How would he keep her from finding out? She would torture him. Pull out his fingernails. Threaten him with hot needles.

No, worse. She'd stare up at him with those big eyes of hers.

Best to nip this in the bud.

He disengaged her arms and stepped away. "It's nothing."

"If it's nothing, why can't you tell me about it?"

"Forget it, okay? It's late and I'm tired."

"We don't keep secrets from each other."

Well, two could play this game. "Oh, really? Like the time you almost got roasted in a furnace? Or the time the mob came after you because you wouldn't stop asking questions? Or the time—"

"You make it sound like all of that was my fault."

"Just leave it be. There's nothing wrong. Nothing you need to know right now."

"Right now? Will you tell me when there is something I need to know?"

He planted a kiss on her forehead. "Of course." He returned to the living room. "I think it's time for bed for all of us. We have an exciting day ahead tomorrow, and a late night, if we're going to catch the eclipse in all its glory."

Bradley hugged him. "Good night, Grampa."

"Night, son. And don't forget your bag over by the door."

"Yes, sir. Night, Gramma."

She gathered the boy into a momma bear sized hug, which he permitted for all of about ten seconds before pulling away. Then he retrieved his bag, telescope, and camera, and headed down the hall to his room.

Carly tidied up the mess on the coffee table while Mike went around the house and checked the doors and turned off lights.

Then they did what he'd hoped to do when he first arrived: called it a night.

As he closed his eyes and waited for sleep, one thing was certain.

He'd have to tell Dr. Nick not to call him again. He would initiate the calls.

Carly's third degree interrogation skills were sharp as claws.

And he didn't want them ripping him apart.

$ $ $

Carly dreamed about an alarm clock going off, but every time she hit the snooze button, it started up again. She sat up in bed and glanced at the clock radio beside her.

Midnight.

Why would the crazy thing be going off now?

Except it wasn't.

The doorbell was.

Beside her, Mike snored through his dreams as usual. Doc stretched out by her feet, and the sheets were a tangled mess she had to extricate herself from.

The bell rang several more times. "I'm coming, I'm coming. Hold onto your horses."

She slid her feet into slippers and shrugged into her housecoat, then trudged down the hallway to the front door. Always cautious—no matter what Mike said—she flicked on the porch light and checked to see who was there.

The journalist from the bus station today.

What did he want?

She was unlikely to find out by keeping the door between them, so she inched the barrier open, wedging her foot behind in case he tried to hurl himself into her house. "What is it?"

"Sorry to bother you. And I know it's late. Can I come in?"

She clutched the neck of her robe closer around her neck. "No, you cannot. My family is asleep. What do you want?"

"I've been poking around town, and everybody tells me you are the best solver of mysteries in the county. Maybe even the state. You help the police all the time, usually figuring out whodunit before they do. Is that right?"

As flattering as his words might be at some other time—such as noon rather than midnight—she needed her sleep. "And this brings you to my house in the wee hours of the morning because?"

"I've discovered a mystery I think you might be interested in."

"Why?"

He blinked a couple of times, the whites of his eyes yellowish from the light overhead. "Like I said, I talked to a couple of people. Background for my story, you know. And one thing led to another, and someone told me about this guy, so I went to talk to his neighbors, and—"

She shuffled from one foot to the other. "No, I mean why do you think I'd be interested?"

"Oh. Well, it's got to do with a secret. And money. And did I mention a secret?"

"Mr. Paulson, you really need to work on your presentation skills. Excuse me, but it's midnight."

She closed the door then lifted the lace curtain in the sidelight window to make sure he left.

He stared at the door for a long moment, and she thought maybe he'd ring the bell again.

But he didn't.

Instead, his shoulders drooped and his chin dropped to his chest, and he retraced his steps on her walkway until he reached his car parked at the curb. She waited. He got in, started the engine, and pulled away.

As the exhaust from his car evaporated, she wondered if she'd done the right thing. Maybe she should have asked a few questions. He seemed disappointed she wasn't interested.

She stepped away from the window. But really, it was midnight, for crying out loud.

There was nothing he had to say that couldn't wait until tomorrow.

It's not like it was a matter of life and death.

Wednesday, October 27th

Chapter 3

12:15 p.m.

Carly snuck a peak at the clock on her desk. Her stomach rumbled like an old Model T chugging up a hill. Almost time for lunch. Across the desk, Mike pecked away at his keyboard. Tap, tap, tap. Delete. Delete. Tap. Tap.

She tossed a paperclip in his direction. Vaguely. It bounced off his computer screen and disappeared over the edge of his desk.

He paused, fingers poised over the keyboard. "We should hire you out to the Yankees."

She grinned. "The Red Sox are your favorite team."

"I know. With that arm, they'd never beat Boston again."

This time she threw her pencil, which caught him eraser-end-first in the center of his chest before falling to the floor. He gripped his shirt, eyes rolling up, a moan escaping his lips that would rival that of the *Mystery Theater* woman on the roof.

She giggled at his display of theatrics. "If you ever decide to give up programming, you should think about soap operas."

One side of his mouth lifted. "It's all fun and games until somebody gets their eye poked out with a sharp stick."

"No danger of that. According to you, I couldn't hit the broad side of a barn." She snapped her fingers. "Oh, wait, I was trying to hit the broad side of a barn, and I got you instead. Talk about luck." She flicked off her monitor. "I'm going to get lunch. Did Bradley say when he'd be back?"

Mike turned his attention back to his work. "Nope. I told him by noon, though. Didn't want him hanging around and making a nuisance of himself."

A tiny knot of concern germinated in her gut. "It's twenty past noon now. Would you go and check on him? See if he's coming up the road?"

"Let's give him until half past. You go ahead and get something going, and I'll finish this last email then go outside."

It was now her turn to roll her eyes. One last email. That could take anywhere from a minute to an hour. But pestering didn't get her anywhere, and asking more than three times was nagging, at least in Mike's thesaurus, so she dropped it.

Fifteen minutes and three bacon, tomato, and lettuce sandwich-preparations later, and Carly returned to the office. "Lunch is ready, and Bradley is late. Do you think he could have gotten lost?"

"I doubt it." Mike stood and stretched. "Can lunch wait while we go look?"

"Sure." That tiny worry knot doubled in size. "He's probably coming up the street now."

"I'm sure you're right."

She gripped his hand tight as they locked the front door and headed down Jamaica Street, toward Old Tom's Hill, and turned right on Main Street. Vans proclaiming a myriad of television and radio stations lined both sides of the street, consuming over half of the regulation parking spaces. Jacob Roy's gas station overflowed with vehicles parked all around the building, and the church parking lot looked like it did during the summer social—cars and trucks and motorhomes parked in every direction on the lawn, in the field, and, of course, in the parking lot.

But still no sign of Bradley.

They crossed the street to check with Jacob, the last of one of the original founding families of the town. They found him pumping gas for a customer. No self-serve foolishness for him. At least, that's what he always said.

Carly nodded to him in the tradition greeting of Down Easterners. "Hi Jacob."

"Ayuh, Miss Carly." He quirked his chin toward Mike. "Good thing you're here with her, Mike. Beautiful woman like that wouldn't be safe on the streets during a time like this."

Despite believing his compliments were as phony as his tall tales of the town, his words still brought a rush of heat to her cheeks. "Thanks, Jacob. Seen Bradley today?"

"Ayuh."

He chewed on a toothpick, his trademark affectation.

Hope rose in Carly like a hot air balloon.

"This mornin'. 'Bout nine or so." He pointed toward the harbor. "Thataway. Said somethin' about findin' a good van-tage point to see the eclipse." He chuckled. "Told him anywhere comfortable would do, since the moon would be over the whole town. No point spending time and energy since nowhere would be better than 'nother."

Her balloon dropped like it was made of lead. "You haven't seen him since?"

"No, Missy. That I haven't." He shook his head as the pump clicked off. He returned the handle and replaced the gas cap. "Been a mite busy, though, as you can see."

Mike squeezed her arm. "Bradley said he was going to the park. And if he came back this way, he'd be home by now."

"Maybe he's already home."

He shook his head. "We'd have to pass him. And we didn't."

"Maybe you should go home in case he comes back another way. I'd hate for him to return to an empty house."

Another shake. "I'm going with you. We can split up and search both sides of the street that way."

This made sense to her mystery-lover's mind and her grandmother's heart.

"Okay. You take the other side."

He hugged her. "You must be really worried."

She pulled away and looked up at him. "Should I be?"

"No. I think the boy is fine. But if you don't want to go into the bakery, you're worried."

Maybe he was right. Rarely did she pass the establishment without indulging in some delectable delight.

But today her mind was elsewhere.

After agreeing to meet at the Blossom Street entrance to the park, Mike trotted across the street. Carly crossed Roy Street and headed for the grocery store, where the shelves were almost as bare as when a hurricane was forecast for the area. Next came the radio station and flower shop, but neither Molly at KWCV nor Bud of Bloomin' Buds recalled seeing him that day.

Mrs. Olsen at the pharmacy saw him passing on her side of the street earlier, but wasn't sure of the time. "Before the rush of traffic into town, to be sure."

When pressed, she thought that was past nine.

Which confirmed what Jacob told them.

To thank the older woman for the information, Carly purchased Bradley's favorite comic book as a welcome home present.

At the town hall building, Mrs. Bailes shook her head when asked if she'd seen the boy. "Not today. Expect he'll be in, though. Always pops in to say hi. Polite young man."

Carly agreed with her and headed across the hallway to the police department. Chief Donovan wasn't in, but Claudia the dispatcher said she'd put out the word to watch for Bradley.

And last but not least, a quick stop at Evie Mack's desk confirmed she'd not seen the boy either. Or if she had, she didn't recall, since she came in early and hadn't set foot outside her office all day.

Although itching to continue into the town park in search of her grandson, Carly waited for Mike at the gate, spotting another familiar face first. Joe, her former boss, looked older every time she saw him. He paused to chat for a minute while walking his dog, a Jack Russell named, of all things, Jack. The pup bounced on the end of his leash like a rubber ball. He hadn't seen Bradley yet today, and she waved him off on his errand, always glad she'd found him in that furnace.

A couple of families passed her by, one going into the park, and the other exiting. Every time a child called out, her gramma senses went on high alert. After a few minutes of heart-pounding joy and gut-wrenching disappointment, she sat on an iron bench, wishing she could do more.

She could call the police chief and report Bradley as missing. She could call Tom and Sarah, but they couldn't do anything right now except worry. And she'd much rather find him than admit she couldn't retain custody of her nine-year-old grandson. She could— what else could she do than what she was doing? Which was wait for Mike to complete his search of the other side of the street.

If he had no news, they'd walk around the park. No doubt their grandson simply lost track of time. They'd find him on top of a hill, or down near the harbor on the beach. Or out on the quay. Or up in a tree.

But what if they didn't?

Maybe somebody snatched him.

Maybe he fell in the water.

Maybe he fell asleep in somebody's shed and got locked in and now those people left town for a month and he'd be so scared and wouldn't have anything to eat or drink or—

"Stop it."

She snapped her head toward the source of the command.

Mike. Standing before her, arms folded over his chest, his brow drawn down.

"Stop what?"

"You've got your grandson dead in a ditch."

"Not true."

"Or drowned in a puddle of water. Or locked in a cellar."

Close, but not quite—she sighed. "You know me too well."

He pulled her close. "Watching your face was like seeing a movie. All of those scenarios passed by. Never play poker. You'll give away your hand every time."

She slipped her arm around his waist. "How do we think like a preteen? Where would he go?"

"He said he wanted to find a good place to see the eclipse. Not in the woods. Not near the town. Somewhere else."

"Like on the hill?"

"Let's start there."

About a quarter mile into the park, the path split, with one arm going down to the water, the other up a steep incline to an open field that overlooked both town and harbor.

Huffing and puffing after about the first hundred feet, Carly persevered. Finding her grandson safe and sound was worth the extra effort, although she subscribed to the idea that everybody was assigned a certain number of heartbeats, and wasting them on exercise ensured a shortened life.

But since this wasn't truly exercise for exercise sake, perhaps she'd get a bye this one time.

At the top, they walked the perimeter of the clearing, calling to Bradley. After each hail, they paused to listen.

But the only response came from the gulls hovering on the air currents and a dog on a sailboat.

Carly cupped her hands around her mouth. "Bradley. Come out. Don't worry. You're not in trouble."

Mike duplicated her efforts with his booming voice.

Still nothing.

40

At the edge of the woods, something blue caught her eye.

Bradley left the house that morning wearing blue jeans.

Her breath caught in her throat on a lump the size of Texas. She pointed. "Mike. Look."

He pressed her arm. "Stay here."

He stepped over the edge into the thick underbrush, slipping on the damp soil, grabbing a couple of saplings to steady himself.

When Carly followed, he glanced up. "I said stay there."

She stopped. "You might need help."

"If I do, I'll let you know."

"You might not know you need my help."

"I'll know."

She waited, sweat dripping down her back. A mosquito buzzed around her face, and she swatted it away, but it returned a moment later with two of its friends. Keeping her eyes glued to Mike's movement down the bank, she stilled herself long enough for all three to light on her arm, when she promptly flattened them with a single slap.

Mike's head snapped around, and she shrugged. He continued his downward descent.

At the bottom, he pulled aside a bush and stepped through the opening. She followed his line of travel, pausing at the tip of a tennis shoe poking out of the leaves that littered the floor of the woods.

Bradley wore tennis shoes that morning, too.

But were they brown, like these?

Or red?

Seemed he wore red ones yesterday.

But he might have two pairs.

A scream welled up inside her, and black dots danced at the edges of her periphery.

She dug her fingernails into her palms.

This wasn't Bradley.

It couldn't be.

She wouldn't let it be.

$ $ $

Mike crept up on the sight before him, hoping this was all some sick joke. It wasn't Bradley, he could see that now. But that didn't mean this wasn't still serious.

A man. Middle-aged, judging by the bald spot on the back of his head where his crown used to be. And where an open wound the size of an orange now revealed blood and bone and—and more.

He swallowed hard. Why did his wife always manage to get mixed up in these things?

And where was his grandson?

He paused about two feet from the body. Because body it surely was. The head, resting with its left cheek on the ground, bore wide, staring, sightless eyes. A trickle of blood ran down its cheek like a ghastly scar, leaving a trail of congealed liquid that browned at the edges. The hands, clenched into fists, attached to outstretched arms, and legs akimbo, gave the distinct impression this man simply fell where he was hit.

And there, not five feet away, a rock about the size of a cantaloupe, colored by something reddish-brown. A leaf stuck to the stain like an attempt at camouflage, but more likely the result of the errant breeze that lifted the litter on the woods floor and stirred it like a witch's brew.

At a footfall behind him, he whirled about, fists ready to defend himself.

Carly, her face white, eyes wide, stared past him.

He hastened to reassure her. "It's not Bradley."

She exhaled, and her knees looked like they were ready to give out beneath her. "Thank God."

Agreeing but not sure where that took them, he caught her by the arm. "Sit over here on that log. I'll call the police."

She followed his directions, which in and of itself was a miracle. A sure sign she was in shock. She eased down onto the fallen tree and put her head between her knees.

He patted her back. "Are you going to be okay?"

She nodded, her head still down. "I was so afraid it was—"

"I know. Me, too."

"I kept thinking how I was going to tell Tom and Sarah—" She hiccupped, a sure sign she was trying really hard not to cry. "I'm sorry. I've found my share of bodies, but it's a lot more personal when I thought it was somebody I knew."

He pulled his phone from a pocket and dialed. "You've found *more* than your share of bodies, by the way. And I know what you— hi, Claudia. Mike Turnquist. Can you send the chief to the park? We found a body near the path leading to the playing field."

"Carly with you?"

"Yes, Claudia. Carly is here."

"Figures. That woman is a walking cadaver hound."

It was one thing for him to think—and even say—that about his wife, but another for somebody else to confirm his errant thoughts. "I found the body this time."

"One moment." A couple of clicks on the line before the dispatcher returned. "Chief is on his way. ETA two minutes. Give or take. Do we need an ambulance?"

"He's past needing medical attention."

"Okey dokey. And tell Carly I put out an APB on Bradley. No sign of him yet?"

"No. Thanks, Claudia." Mike disconnected the call and returned his phone to his pocket. "Claudia says she put out the call on Bradley."

"Good." Carly raised her head and straightened, swiping her fingers through her hair. Her cheeks were stained with tears, and her reddened eyes welled with more. She stood and brushed off her jeans. "I need to keep looking."

He pressed her back to her makeshift seat. "You need to stay here with me until the chief says it's okay to go."

"But Bradley—"

"We'll find him."

Sirens echoed through the trees, drawing nearer and more strident. A few minutes later, and Chief Donovan slid down the incline, sweat dotting his upper lip.

He paused, surveyed the scene, and nodded to Mike. "Which way did you approach?"

Mike pointed. "Just about where you are. I went around that tree when I realized it was a body."

Donovan nodded toward Carly. "And you?"

"The same."

"Good. At least you haven't mucked up the crime scene too badly. Can you retrace your steps?"

Mike nodded. "We can. And we will." He took Carly's hand. "Come on. You can do this."

She nodded and licked her lips. "Yes, we can."

Mike turned to the chief. "We'll wait up on the field."

"I'll be up shortly."

Mike held Carly's now-cold-and-clammy hand in his and half-pulled, half-dragged her from the woods, back up the embankment, and onto the playing field. The sun warmed the air, brightening the gloom that threatened to drown them down in the underbrush.

A set of wooden bleachers sat just off the edge of the field, and he led her there. After brushing off a spot, she sat, exhaling as she did. She wrapped her arms around herself as though chilled, and he wished he'd thought to bring a jacket. Or a sweater. Or a blanket.

Except he never expected to find a body in the woods.

Not Bradley's. And not this stranger's.

He narrowed his eyes and peered at his wife. "You're right, you know."

She turned hollow eyes on him. "What do you mean?"

"You tried to tell me you don't go looking for bodies. And it's no fun to find them. But you seem to be such a magnet for them." He patted her shoulder, and she leaned into his touch. "But now I see what you mean. I'll never accuse you of that again."

"I guess one good thing came out of this mess then."

Two o'clock came and went, and still the chief didn't reappear. The black station wagon from the mortuary in Riverdale pulled onto the field, and two men donned coveralls, masks, gloves, and booties, then made their way into the woods bearing their evidence kits. About twenty minutes later, they reappeared, a body bag between them which they placed on a gurney and rolled toward the rear of the car.

A couple of minutes later, Chief Donovan topped the rise and waved them over.

Carly exhaled. "Finally. Now maybe he'll let us continue looking for Bradley."

"We might need to give our statement first."

"No. First we need to find our grandson."

Her chin jutted out.

Mike was glad he wasn't the one to tell her otherwise.

The chief paused beside the gurney, and Mike and Carly joined him. He turned to Mike first. "Did you recognize him?"

"No. I was too busy staring at his open eyes, I guess. And the wound. And the rock."

"Understandable." He turned to Carly. "And you?"

"Mike wouldn't let me get close enough."

The chief unzipped the body bag. "Don't touch anything, but take a look and let me know if you know him."

Mike glanced at the man then shook his head. The man's blue lips and pale face unnerved him, and he stood aside to allow Carly to peer at the face while he took a couple of deep breaths to clear his head.

One quick look, and they'd be out of here.

Carly gasped. "Oh, no. I know this man."

Then again, maybe not.

$ $ $

Why couldn't she have kept her big mouth shut? If she simply said she didn't know him, she and Mike could have continued searching for Bradley.

But no—she had to go and blurt out the last thing Mike wanted to hear right now.

Both men stared at her. Well, maybe Mike's look was more of a glare.

The chief cleared his throat. "How do you know him?"

No point trying to back-peddle. Best to come right out with the truth and get it over with. "He's a journalist. In town to cover the eclipse. His name is Harvey Paulson."

"Television or radio?"

She kept her gaze fixed on Donovan. "Newspaper."

"Which one?"

Carly tried to visualize his business card. Which he showed but never actually gave her. She shook her head. "I can't remember. He put the card back into his shirt pocket."

"He kept it?"

"He did."

"And you didn't think this was suspicious because?"

"Because I didn't want to know this odious man. He was taking pictures of Bradley and me—" She inhaled sharply. "Do you think he had anything to do with Bradley's disappearance?" She clenched her fists. "If so, I'll—"

The chief peered at her. "You'd do what? Kill him? I think somebody beat you to the punch."

She drew a couple of breaths. This was getting out of hand. And fast. "No, I didn't mean that. At least, not literally. I told him he didn't have my permission to print pictures of either of us. He said he was doing a human interest story about the town and the eclipse, and I told him to take it somewhere else."

The chief made a few notes in a small pad. "See him again?"

She'd come clean so far. What was the point in saying anything about Harvey's late-night visit? She hadn't let him in. He hadn't told her anything.

Mike squeezed her hand. "What aren't you telling us?"

"Nothing."

And it was nothing, wasn't it? She straightened her shoulders. "I had no reason to see him again. He knew where I stood regarding the story."

There. Not exactly a lie.

The chief studied her a moment, his mouth opening a couple of times as though to say something, then snapping shut. She held her breath. If he pressed her, she'd likely cave like a house of cards.

He nodded. "If you think of anything else, let me know." He turned to the two forensic technicians. "You can take him away."

They rolled the gurney to the rear of the wagon, released the catch, and slid the works into the car. After removing their crime scene garb, they got into the vehicle and headed back to the maintenance road at the end of the field.

The chief turned to Carly. "By the way, we found something clutched in his hand." He pulled a paper evidence bag from his jacket pocket and extracted a piece of paper, holding it with two fingers on one corner. "Know this man?"

Carly straightened out the crumpled item inside the bag. "Sure, it's Mayor Akerman. Everybody knows him."

"So how does a two-bit stringer from out of town know the mayor? And why would he have this photo clutched in his dead, lifeless hand?"

Carly forced a smile. "Well, Chief Donovan, I guess it's why the town pays you the big bucks. To answer those tough questions."

The man harrumphed, tucked the photo into the bag and the bag into his pocket, and headed for his patrol car parked at the far end of the field. Halfway there, he paused and turned around.

Carly's breath hitched in the back of her throat. Would he push her story? Beat her with a rubber hose until she confessed?

"Stay out of it, Carly."

Then he turned, reached his car, slid into the driver's seat, turned off the emergency lights, and drove away, leaving nothing more than a small cloud of exhaust as evidence of his presence.

That, and Carly's racing heart.

$ $ $

Bradley was scared.

More than at any other time in his life.

More than the time his dad was arrested and he had to hide in the back seat of their car, covered by a blanket, while the car was towed to the police impound lot.

More than when that stupid kid threatened to punch out his lights.

Even way more when Grampa Mike and Gramma Carly told him

his daddy was dead.

He huddled in the corner of the shed and peered through the gloom. Already he'd called for help until his voice went hoarse, not much more than a whisper.

And still nobody came.

He'd pounded on the doors and the walls until he had splinters and sore hands.

And still nobody came.

Maybe nobody ever would.

Maybe he'd die here, in this shed.

Is that what the man wanted?

The one who chased him through the woods and grabbed him?

He should have run faster.

He should have fought harder.

He should have screamed louder.

But he didn't.

And here he was, locked in, the only light coming from a few spaces between the boards.

Spaces not wide enough to get his fingers between. He already tried.

And had broken off his nails and got more splinters.

He sucked at his sore knuckles, wishing he had something to drink.

Would the man come back?

His captor's face flashed in front of him. Stern eyes. Thin lips. Bad breath.

Fist raised as though to hit him.

Well, he wasn't afraid of getting hit.

His first father beat him lots. Left bruises, too.

No, that wasn't what scared him the most.

What scared him the most—what took his breath away—was being left here alone.

Forever.

Chapter 4

2:30 p.m.

Carly sighed. Sometimes the accountant in her drove her almost to distraction. Counting everything. From cars in traffic to beans in her soup pot.

Okay. She didn't go quite that far.

Then people really would call her a bean counter.

But that didn't stop her from counting the rings until her son answered his phone. Why did folks carry a cell if they didn't intend to take calls?

She glanced at the clock. Three hours earlier in LA. Would Tom still be at work? Or in the hotel?

A click on the other end, and, expecting she reached his voice mail, she launched into her message. "Tom, it's Carly. Can you call me? It's really important."

"Hey, Carly. Sounds serious. Give me a second while I leave the room." Muffled voices and shifting chairs covered the blank space of several seconds. "Okay. In the hallway now. What? No hello? No 'how is life on the West Coast'?"

He chuckled, sounding so much like his father. Which, under normal circumstances, would cheer her. But not today.

"Sorry, Tom. Thought I got your messaging system."

"So what's got you so all-fired upset? And don't 'nothing' me. I hear it in your voice. And your words."

She sighed. Like his father, he knew her too well. There'd be no beating around the bush on this one. "Bradley's wandered off.

Wanted to let you know before you heard it from somewhere else."

"Wandered off? Heard it from somewhere else? What does that mean?"

Noting the lowering of his voice and the dropping of his jocularity, she chose her words carefully. "He went for a walk this morning. Said he was looking for the perfect vantage point for watching the eclipse tonight."

"And?"

"Well, that was after breakfast. When he didn't come home for lunch, we knew something was wrong. That child eats more than you do."

"He's probably just wandering around with his head in the clouds. You know how boys can be."

"That's just it. We asked around town, and everybody we talked to saw him heading to the park this morning, but not since. So we followed the way he'd go, and we couldn't find him."

"Do you need us to fly home and help?"

"No, your dad and I are fine for now." How much more should she tell him? If he heard about the journalist's death on the news, her son would blow a gasket that she didn't inform him first. "But Tom, there is one other thing."

"Doesn't sound good."

"We found a body."

"A body?"

"Yes. A reporter in town to cover the eclipse. See, the thing is, we met him yesterday at the bus station."

Now it was Tom's turn to sigh. A great, heaving, persecuted exhalation exactly like his fathers. "Now, why doesn't that surprise me?"

"It's not like I go around looking for—"

"I'm not talking about the body. I mean the fact that you're involved."

"I didn't say I was—"

"You're in the same town. You talked to him. You're involved."

Carly's vision blurred. Mike said the same thing. As if finding the body of a person that she had even a tenuous connection with was her fault. She swallowed past the lump in her throat. "I'm sorry, Tom. This was supposed to be a safe place to send your son."

"Not really your fault. It's just who you are, that's all. And I don't think this unfortunate fellow's death has anything to do with Bradley's disappearance."

Well, that was a relief. Because she certainly didn't think so, either. Even Chief Donovan downplayed Bradley's absence. "Thanks, Tom. But back to Bradley. You don't think he—he—has anything happened recently?"

"Apart from the usual nine-year-old angst?"

"Right. Apart from that."

"He did get into a fight in the school yard about two weeks ago. Something about some kid calling him a nasty name. Bradley had to stay in after school for a week, and the other boy was suspended for two days."

"How did Bradley react to that?"

"He was pretty sore about it. We tried to explain that we need to use our fists to defend ourselves only when our words don't work. Like if a stranger tried to grab him and put him in a car. But in school, we use our words to diffuse the situation because ultimately, these people are our friends and neighbors."

"And what did he say?"

"That this boy wasn't a friend or a neighbor, and that he deserved to be punched." Another sigh. "Sometimes I see so much of Uncle Jerry in him that it scares me."

"Me, too. But you are making a big difference in his life. He has been a delight while he's been here."

"Doesn't sound like that little episode is what's hanging over him."

She hoped he was right, but his behavior was concerning. Perhaps he took advantage of the freedom they granted him—thinking their little town was safe—to run away. After all, it's what his natural father did whenever things got hot or uncomfortable. Which is why when Jerry turned up last year with a son in tow, nobody was convinced of his protestations that he was turning over a new leaf.

Unfortunately, they were all proven correct. Except Jerry did try—too little too late—but he did the right thing by leaving a letter asking Mike to look after his boy.

"Do we need to make our excuses and come back early?"

And what would they say? "Our parents lost our child."

Carly pulled herself back to the present, swallowing down the lump of fear in her gut. "No need. I have a feeling he'll reappear soon. Maybe he made a new friend and went home with them. Or he wandered a little further than he expected." A nice way to say he ran away. "Mike and I will keep looking. The police have alerts out about him. And folks in town know we're missing him. Our next call will be to tell you he's back safe and sound."

"Okay. I'll let Sarah know. She might insist on coming home, but if you think it's a false alarm, I'll try to talk her out of it. She's bogged down in some complicated negotiations right now, but I know she'd drop it in a second if you wanted us there."

"No, we're fine."

She promised to call as soon as they knew anything, then disconnected.

Feeling anything but fine.

$ $ $

Once again, Carly headed downtown, leaving Mike working at home with the sacred promise to call her as soon as Bradley returned home. Everywhere she looked, she sought the child. Every pale headed boy drew her in that direction. Every child of about his height gave her pause.

If he was in town, she'd find him.

And if he wasn't, she'd look further afield. Despite her feigned nonchalance with Tom, certainty grew in her that her grandson wasn't coming home because somebody—or something—prevented him.

Following her talk with Tom, a quick call to Chief Donovan confirmed there'd been no sightings of Bradley, but they were still looking.

His veiled comments indicated she should leave both the missing boy and the dead journalist in professional hands.

Well, she was a professional, wasn't she? Of course she was.

So she could cover both cases.

In fact, all three. Because as busy as she was with the other two, there was still the matter of the missing money. And perhaps all three were connected in some way. Although, right now, she couldn't see how her grandson's disappearance could be related to either a murder or embezzlement.

In fact, she was fairly certain these were three different crimes with three different perpetrators.

Not that Bradley's disappearance was a crime. No, that was simply too horrible to contemplate.

So, in reality, she had one mystery, one conundrum, and one crime.

A missing boy, missing money, and murder.

What a combination.

She headed downtown, taking careful note of everything and

everybody she passed.

Take, for example, the bank. Just last year, it was the site of a fake robbery that almost destroyed her reputation. Not likely anybody working there had lured a child in with candy or killed a newspaper man. Still, she made a mental note to check in on her way back.

Past the bank, the bakery oozed tempting sweet smells. The Sweet Tooth was pumping out the pecan tarts again today. No, she'd resist for now, but appeased her rumbling stomach with a promise to stop in there on the way home, too. And ask about Bradley. And Harvey Paulson. Maybe he'd been in the shop. Paulson, that was.

She waved to Margaret at the Snip 'n Clip, and nodded to a couple exiting the Dew Drop Inn, doggie bags in hand. No doubt about it, that place knew how to stuff a body. Had her grandson gone in there to beg some lunch? Another mental note to ask later.

After looking both ways on the now-busy Main Street, she dodged a couple of cars and walked up the steps to the library/town hall. Upstairs, she paused in front of Evie Mack's desk and waited until the secretary paused in her typing. When asked how she could be helped, Carly had her answer ready. "I was hoping to have a few words with the members of the council."

Evie smiled up at her, but a knot between her eyebrows indicated everything wasn't peachy keen in her world. "They aren't here today. The next meeting isn't for a few weeks. They all hold jobs, you know, outside of their service to the town."

"Oh, I hadn't thought of that. Do you know where I might find them?"

"Well, Bob is a paramedic, so likely either at the fire station or the community hospital. Anita is a nurse at the hospital. And Gail operates a salon from her home."

"Great, thanks."

Two minutes later, Carly pushed through the office door into the fire station that shared the same building with the town hall and library. Off to the right, a shiny red—if slightly older—fire engine occupied the single bay. Thankfully, Bear Cove needed little more since all the buildings were one story except for this one, and the town had never been plagued with conflagrations such as New York, Boston, and Chicago experienced.

Also thankfully, Bob Whalen was in the station, checking supplies in the rear of the only other vehicle in the station, the ambulance.

She perched on the tailgate and observed him a while until he glanced her way. "Hi, Bob. We met last year at the Fourth of July picnic."

He tossed her a smile. "I remember. Carrie, isn't it? Any news on your grandson?"

She gritted her teeth. *Yes, Bill.* "Carly. And no. But we're sure we'll find him soon. He couldn't have gotten far."

He turned his attention to a small cardboard box of items he unpacked into a built-in drawer. "This is a safe town." He chuckled. "Well, maybe not so safe for that journalist fellow." He peered at her. "Say, you found him, didn't you?"

"Yes. It was horrible."

"'Spect so. Most folks aren't accustomed to finding bodies." He chuckled. "'Cept you, of course."

"It's not like I went looking for a body."

"I know. A regular Jessica Fletcher, you are."

Despite his reference to one of her heroes in the mystery world, the skin on the back of her neck prickled. Something was off about this guy.

He picked up another box. "Mind if I keep working? Might get a call, and I like to be ready."

She waggled her fingers in his direction. "Go right ahead. Mind if *I* work while *you* work?"

He paused and glanced at her. "Don't understand."

"Mayor hired me to do an audit of the town books."

"Thought the town already had an auditor."

"It does." She shifted on her perch. Time to come up with a company line, of sorts. "Call this a pre-audit. He wants to make sure everything is top-top before the formal audit."

"And what do you want from me?"

"As town manager, you have access to both the bank accounts and the financial records."

His face turned red. "You implying I took something?"

Interesting question. Why would he automatically assume something was missing? Guilty conscience? Or too many mystery books? Not that she knew for certain what genre he read. "Not at all. No. I was just wondering if any of the accounting practices changed in the last six months or so?"

"You mean beside the election of Akerman?"

"No love lost there, I see."

Bob set aside the clear plastic container of bandages and tape. "He's a smarmy used car salesman who thinks he has all the answers to all the questions. Likes to make changes for change's sake."

She tipped her head in question. "I thought he was a realtor."

"I meant in aptitude if not profession."

"Gotcha. Seems like he cares about the town, though."

"Perhaps. Native boy moved to the big city, made good, came back with money in his pocket and pedigree on his side."

Say what you really think, Bob. "In what ways has the mayor made changes?"

"Usually behind the scenes, under the table, or over objection." Bob shook his head. "Don't know why he bothers to even include us in his decisions. He never listens. Never thinks we might know more about any subject than he does. He's been loose with town funds. I suggest you start with him."

"Start with him?"

"If anything is missing."

This wasn't making any sense. "Why would he hire me to look for a discrepancy if he's responsible for it?"

Bob's mouth lifted in a half-smile. "Best way to cover his tracks, right? I mean, you start out with the notion he can't be responsible, so you look elsewhere. Did he say how much is missing?"

Time to redirect the conversation. "So nothing's different in how you recognize assets and income? No change in fiscal year? Or alteration of depreciation schedules? No mysterious charges going through the books?"

He closed his eyes a moment then opened them and shook his head. "Nope."

A piercing bell rang, setting firemen sliding down the pole and hurrying to the engine.

Bob stood. "Gotta go."

"Thanks for your help." She stood as he stepped to the floor beside her, barely moving out of the way before he slammed the door shut. "If I have any other questions—"

"You know where to find me."

He moved out of sight as the oversized garage doors opened, then the ambulance engine roared to life, and both vehicles eased out of the building.

Well, that was that. Not real informative, but definitely gave the impression of barely disguised animosity between at least Bob and the mayor.

An interesting tidbit, that.

Not to mention he seemed to be less than forthcoming with

information apart from how much he disliked the mayor.

His reticence spoke volumes.

Next, she headed for Anita's home, which sat at the end of Second Street and bordered the park. After that, she planned to check in at the community hospital, which would be the next stop on her tour of the town today.

All the while keeping her eyes open for her grandson.

She waved at Jacob Roy who emerged from his garage, wiping his hands on a rag. Jacob responded with that traditional Down East acknowledgment: a sideways dip of the head and a click of the tongue out one side of his mouth.

The climb up Captain Frank's Lane left her breathing hard by the time she reached Anita's gate, so she paused and studied the house a moment. A tidy but small front yard granted the house a larger and more private back area. Split rail fence in the front, six-foot privacy fence in the rear. Mature trees. Shutters that needed painting after the last hail storm went through. Two cars parked in the driveway. A garage behind the fence. A small sign in the front door said MASSAGE. So the woman operated a small business on the side.

Once she breathed easy, she slipped the latch on the gate and walked up to the house. She knocked on the door, which pushed open at her touch. "Anita? Are you there?" When she got no answer, she stepped into the foyer, her arrival announced by a soft pinging somewhere in a room down the hall. The eye-watering combination smells of coconut oil and some kind of herbal oil greeted her. A single-cup coffee maker—still an avant garde luxury in Bear Cove— occupied a cart in a small alcove lined with empty chairs. Various beauty magazines lay scattered on a coffee table.

She waited a moment, not quite sure what the protocol was regarding barging into a home business without an appointment or even the intention of receiving services.

Before she made a decision of what to do, a door at the end of the hall opened, and Anita came toward her, an older woman hobbling alongside, her feet encased in cheap plastic flip-flops.

Carly cringed. She couldn't wear those torture devices, and didn't understand how anybody could. Simply thinking about the rigid piece of rubber jammed between her toes sent her shuddering.

But she controlled both her feelings and her facial expression. At least, that's what the mirror over the coffee maker confirmed.

She deserved an Academy Award.

The customer continued toward the door, and Carly stepped aside, averting her gaze from the woman's footwear. She'd rather find a hundred bodies than endure that poor dear's travail.

Anita studied her. "Did you have an appointment? If not, I could squeeze you in."

Not into those shoes, you couldn't.

Carly pasted on her most professional smile. "No appointment. I don't know if you remember me. Carly Turnquist. We met at the restaurant the other day? With Mrs. Bailes?"

"Oh, yes." Anita glanced at her wristwatch. Rather pointedly. "Well, you caught me between clients."

"I didn't know you offered massages."

"Just on my days off. It's word of mouth, really. Just trying to make a little extra money."

"Right. Would you have a few minutes? I need to talk to you about the town's financial records."

Anita's face paled. "I have a customer in hot wraps. I don't have—"

"Just a few questions."

The woman glanced at her watch. Again. "Five. No more."

No time for niceties today. Feeling as though Anita already counted down the seconds, Carly plunged in. "The mayor asked me to do a kind of pre-audit on the town's books."

"Is there money missing?"

Interesting that two people asked the same question.

"Not sure. I wanted to ask if you noticed anything different about the way monies were handled recently?"

Anita's eyes narrowed. "You might want to look at a couple of contracts the mayor approved without putting them out for bids. And several expenses which might be—how should I say it?—not quite kosher."

"Thank you for your candidness. Anything else?"

A baby cried from a room on the right. Anita stiffened but never took her eyes off Carly. Which was strange.

In for a penny, in for a pound, as her grandmother used to say.

Carly nodded toward the sound. "Do you need to check on her?"

"Him. And no."

"A boy. How nice. How old is he?"

"Four months."

"What a delightful age. Every day something new." Carly took a step toward the room. "Sure you don't need to check on him?"

"Positive."

"I feel really silly calling him, him. What's his name?"

"JW."

"Delightful. Initials. Short for something else?"

"Yes." Anita wrung her fingers together into knots. "If there's nothing else?"

"How do you get along with the other members of the council?"

She shrugged. "Gail is a nice lady. Works hard as treasurer. Bob is dedicated. A family man. Committed to his children."

"And his wife?"

"And his wife."

Which left Mayor Akerman conspicuously absent.

"And the mayor?"

She lifted one shoulder and dropped it. "Fine."

Funny how that single word could be interpreted in so many ways.

Carly stepped toward the door. "Well, I'll let you get back to work. Thanks for your time. If I have more questions—"

"Please call."

Not exactly the response she hoped for.

Seemed like Anita might have something to hide.

That made two. Bob Whalen and her.

Interesting.

$ $ $

A quick jog down the lane and back up Main Street then up Roy Street—well, not exactly a jog, since Carly thought it a ploy of the sneaker industry to sell more shoes—and she arrived at the snug bungalow across the street from the Bear Cove Community Hospital.

The house sat back from the road, rose bushes lining the walkway. A skillfully painted sign advertised Gail's occupation—manicures and pedicures. Carly glanced at her hands. Maybe she should take better care of herself. After all, just because she worked from home didn't mean she needed to let herself go completely.

She nibbled at a hangnail. Who was she kidding? She might come once, then tomorrow she'd chew off the polish, break a nail opening a can of cat food, and stub her toe on the leg of the bed. And there would go all her hard-earned money.

She shook her head as she paused on the landing. No, manicures and pedicures were for others, like her former friend Susan. And her not-so-friendly friend Anita, who, despite her occupation, sported lovely nails and designer clothes.

As she pondered whether to walk in or ring the doorbell, a young woman with a delightful head of reddish-blonde curls and a smattering of freckles spanning the bridge of her nose came to the screen door. "Can I help you?"

Carly scanned the name tag on the woman's smock. *Gail Sullivan.* She quickly introduced herself and the reason for her visit, noting how Gail's smile slipped away, replaced by a slight narrowing of the eyes and hardening of the mouth, at the mention of financial records and an audit.

Every time she caught a reaction like that, her first thought was *what is she hiding?*

The manicurist stood as though rooted in the doorway. "I can't help you."

Interesting choice of words. *Can't* often implied more knowledge than the speaker wanted to give.

At least in her experience.

Carly adopted her most persuasive tone—the one which implied that all information, no matter how seemingly irrelevant, could help her out of a jam imposed by someone higher up the management chain. She leaned in closer, almost whispering through the screen. "Personally, I think the mayor is talking out of his hat. But he's hired me to do a job, and if I don't give him something—anything—I don't get paid." She lifted one shoulder and let it drop. "And if I don't get paid, well, that's not good for business."

She tossed the woman a half smile and let the silence build.

After about two minutes, Gail nodded. "The only thing I know is that there's been a lot of tension in the council meetings. Snide comments from Anita about Akerman not knowing what a promise is because he never kept one."

"What do you think that's about?"

"Don't know. There are rumors all over town hall that they had an affair that ended just over a year ago."

Carly gasped. "But the mayor is married."

Gail leaned forward, closing the distance between them. "That doesn't stop most men."

"Any mention of the child?"

Gail shook her head. "No. Don't think it's Akerman's, though."

"What gave you that impression? The timing could be right."

"Maybe. But I also heard she's been seen stepping out with Bob Whalen recently."

"You think he could be the father?"

"Who knows? Amongst the women in this town—married and

unmarried—Anita doesn't have a very good reputation."

An older woman in a similarly-colored smock stuck her head around the corner. "Gail, if you have a minute, could you check on Mrs. White? She says her nails are dry and she needs to leave."

Gail nodded. "Right on it." She looked to Carly. "Sorry I can't help more."

Carly retraced her steps home and pondered her conversation with the less-than-willing councilor. Not sure what information was important and what was peripheral, she headed for the Sweet Tooth Bakery.

She needed to feed her brain cells if she was going to figure out truth from innuendo. From personal experience, insinuations often provided the best rabbit trails—or the worst, depending on the perspective.

She had neither the time nor the inclination to get lost on a tangent.

She had missing money and a grandson to find.

And definitely not in that order.

$ $ $

At the sound of the front door opening, Mike left his office and headed for the living room. Maybe Bradley found his way home after all.

But instead of a nine-year-old boy, his fifty-something wife greeted him. "Hey." She looped her arms around his neck and pulled him close, a brown paper bag clutched in one hand. "No news?"

He shook his head.

She slumped against his chest. "I say we go look for him again. The police don't seem to be doing much."

"Now, Carly."

She opened the bag, revealing pecan tarts nestled in layers of waxed paper. "Brought you a treat."

He took the bag and set it aside. "Don't try to distract me with sweets."

She raised her brows and jabbed a thumb into her chest. "Moi?"

"And don't try your best Miss Piggy on me, either."

Her bottom lip jutted out. "Well, they haven't found him, have they? I mean, how hard can it be to locate one boy in a town of less than four hundred people?"

"Make that more than seven hundred, by conservative estimates. I've been listening to the radio while you're out gallivanting around town. More tourists are flocking into town. Apparently the rest of the eastern seaboard is forecast to have clouds and rain tonight, which makes Bear Cove prime viewing real estate."

Tears welled in her dark brown eyes, and for a moment he regretted his tone. "What else is the news saying?"

He sighed, knowing he didn't have the news she really wanted to hear. "That Donovan and the other officer are searching every garage, outbuilding, shed, barn, and storm cellar in town. They've called in volunteers, and might bring in dogs."

Now the tears spilled over. "Dogs?" Her lips trembled. "They think he's dead, don't they?"

He pulled her close again. "No. Not cadaver dogs. Search and rescue dogs."

She pulled away and peered up at him. "They think he fell down a well or something?" She swiped at her nose. "Tom and Sarah will kill me if anything happens to him." She sobbed. "Why did I ever let him go out alone?"

"First of all, we're going to find him. Secondly, our kids would never hold you responsible. And finally, Bear Cove is a safe town. Kids walk the streets all the time."

"Well, maybe when you were a kid. But not anymore. Not since I moved to town."

He chuckled. "You can't take responsibility for the crime here. It's a sign of the times."

"Where is he, Mike?"

He patted her back. "I don't know. But we'll find him." He took her hand. "Come on. I've got the television on in the office. Let's see what the update is."

They sat at their desks to view the evening news which, as usual, started with local stories before moving on to regional then national and international.

A hip young man with a thick pomade haircut, long on the top and short on the sides, opened with the lead story. "Our breaking story concerns Bear Cove's boy wonder Mayor Walter Akerman. This afternoon, a source provided evidence that the mayor and his secretary are involved in a sordid affair. You be the judge."

An image of Akerman and Evie covered the screen. Evie stood in a doorway, leaning down to kiss the mayor, who looked up at her.

"Calls to the mayor's office were not answered. More at eleven."

"The search continues for a missing boy. Bradley Turnquist, visiting his grandparents in Bear Cove, went missing this morning. Apparently his goal was the park, but he never made it. The police have called in extra resources and volunteers. If you have any information, please call the Bear Cove Police Department."

"And now on to regional news."

Mike leaned over and flicked off the set. "Not much more than we already knew."

"Seems the media is more interested in a scandal in the mayor's office than in finding our grandson."

"They're just following the story that will generate more buzz."

The telephone rang, and Mike picked up the receiver. "Hi, Chief."

"Can I drop in? I'm right outside your door."

Mike's heart sank to the tips of his toes. "Sure."

He disconnected and headed for the foyer, Carly close on his heels.

"What is it, Mike? Who was that?"

The lump in his throat prevented him from answering. Whatever the chief had to say, they'd get through it together. He gestured to Carly's favorite chair. "Sit there and wait."

"Mike."

He paused. "Please, Carly. Do as I ask. Just this once."

She sat, hands folded in her lap.

He opened the door and the chief entered. "Come in. Have a seat."

Donovan removed his hat and sat on the sofa.

Carly leaned forward. "What is it?"

The chief held up a hand, then retrieved a small square of paper from his jacket pocket. "We looked at the pictures in Harvey Paulson's camera. Most were of the town, a few people, trees, a dog or two." He held out his hand. "And this."

Carly reached forward, her hand shaking. She accepted the picture, stared at it a long moment, then handed it to Mike.

He swallowed hard, not sure he wanted to look.

But knowing he must.

A picture of Bradley, wearing his backpack, carrying his telescope.

In the woods.

$$$

If Bradley thought he was scared before, he was wrong.

Because now he was scared spitless.

Or maybe he was simply thirsty.

He'd not had anything to drink since the man threw him in the shed. Sure, he managed to sleep away part of the afternoon, partly because of boredom, and partly because he was so worried that he was worn out.

And now the entire night stretched before him.

No bed.

No blanket.

No television.

And by the looks of it, no supper.

A scritching sound came from the corner of the shed. Bradley pulled his feet up close and rested his chin on his knees. Was there a wild animal trying to burrow into the shed? Would it eat him? Maybe he'd just disappear, never to be found again, like all those children whose parents put their pictures on milk cartons.

Or maybe he'd just die of fright.

That was possible, wasn't it? Isn't that why kids liked the horror movies?

If he ever got out of here, he'd never ask to see another scary movie as long as he lived.

If he ever got out of here, he'd behave himself. Do his chores. Brush his teeth. Ask to do extra chores, even.

Because surely, he must be here because he did something really wrong.

But what? He racked his brain, trying to come up with something.

But nothing came to mind.

Maybe he was being punished for punching the kid at school? Somebody once told him that God was always watching. That must be it. He did something wrong, and God was making him pay. Just like the kid at school said, *You'll pay for that.*

But that sure didn't sound like the God that Margie talked about last summer. She said God loves everybody. And wants everybody to love Him.

Well, he didn't want to love somebody who would punish him and not even tell him why.

Even his first dad didn't do that.

No, with his first dad, a guy always knew why he was being beaten.

Or slapped.

Or strapped.

Or locked in a closet.

Bradley closed his eyes. This shed was too much like the closets in motels where his dad made him stay when he did his business. With his associates, as he called them. One time, one of those associates beat his father up and stole their clothes, their money, and their car. And his dad passed out on the floor, just inches from the closet. But Bradley couldn't get out to help him. Two days he waited until his dad woke up. Two days with nothing to eat or drink. No bathroom. He had to use a corner of the closet as a toilet.

Bradley glanced around in the darkness. Pretty soon he'd have to find a corner.

He hated that part.

Chapter 5

5:15 p.m.

Carly scooted over to share Mike's chair with him. "So we know he made it to the park. That's where we need to look."

The chief nodded. "Already on it."

Mike peered at the photo again. "I recognize this." He pointed to a tree behind Bradley. "That's along the path leading to where we found the journalist."

Carly snatched the picture back. "I don't know. Trees all look the same to me."

He tapped the photo. "No, I'm sure it is. I remember thinking at the time that that knot hole looked like a leprechaun's face."

"What?" Sometimes her husband's imagination got the better of him. And he said she let hers run wild. Not anything like the leaps and bounds his took. "Not seeing it."

Her husband traced his finger around a darker area of a tree trunk. "Sure. It's right there."

The chief reached for his picture. "What this proves is that Bradley and Paulson were in the woods at the same time. The boy is smiling, looks unharmed, natural-like."

Carly nodded. "So whatever happened—to both of them—happened after this was taken." She quirked her chin in the direction of the picture. "Is there a time stamp?"

"Nope. Just a date. Today's."

Mike sat back in his chair, giving Carly room to move closer. He ran a hand up and down her back. "So where does that leave us?"

"We know Bradley made it to the park, so I'll concentrate our search in that area." Donovan sighed. "Do you have an article of clothing he wore recently? In case we bring in the dogs?"

A knot the size of Texas formed in her gut. She licked dry lips. "Yes. The shirt he wore here on the bus. I'll get it."

The chief stood. "I'll do it." He pulled a gallon-sized plastic zip lock bag from another pocket. "Don't need you contaminatin' the evidence. Confusin' the dog."

"Right." She walked down the hallway and stepped aside to let the chief enter. "It's the blue shirt on the chair."

Chief Donovan turned the bag inside out, slipped it over his hand, and picked up the shirt and sealed it inside the plastic. "Thank you." He paused in the doorway. "We're going to find him."

She nodded, unable to speak.

Her grandson's absence had done the impossible.

Left her without a wisecrack response.

$ $ $

After the chief left, Carly sat a long while in her own chair. Mike headed back to the office to deal with his worry in his own way— with work.

And she dealt with the situation in her way—by turning all the information she knew over and over in her head. After a time, an ache developed between her shoulder blades and between her eyes, and she rose and headed for the kitchen.

When in doubt, eat.

They hadn't had their dinner yet, and it was past seven. Hadn't even eaten the sandwiches she prepared for lunch. Which still sat on the counter. She scraped the food into the trash can and set the plates in the dishwasher.

While pasta boiled and sauce simmered, she called the mayor at home. "Did you see the news?'

His forced laugh chilled her to the bone. "Who hasn't? I'm about ready to disconnect the phone."

"Reporters parked outside your door?"

"You make it sound like I should expect that. Wait a minute." Footsteps across a hardwood floor, then a deep sigh. "Right now, just one van. But I suspect more will be on their way."

"We have a plethora of journalists in town for the eclipse. It's inevitable." She paused as she worked on how to ask what she needed to know, then decided to simply go ahead and get the words out. "Is the story true?"

Muffled words in the background and the unmistakable sounds of a hand over the handset reminded her his wife could be nearby. Then he came back on the line. "No, it's not true. I don't know how you could ask me that."

"Walter, you wouldn't be the first elected official who let his position and his power go to his head." She stirred the sauce. "I had to ask."

"Paula and I've been married almost thirty years. Our marriage is rock solid. Nothing like this ever before."

"And Evie?"

"Gold. No, better. Platinum. Nothing improper between us. No touches. No looks. No innuendoes. In fact, she's engaged and leaving in a few months. Getting married." This time his chuckle sounded a little more relaxed. "I've seen him. He's drop-dead gorgeous."

"Looks can be deceiving."

"Right. She'd trade Mr. Six Pack for a man old enough to be her father. And probably with a paunch to match her dear old Dad's."

If what he said was true, he had a point.

Then again, adultery rarely made sense.

She could check with Evie later on.

The timer for the pasta dinged, and she turned the burner off. Holding the phone against her shoulder, she dumped the spaghetti into the colander and rinsed it with cold water. "What about Anita?"

"What about her?"

"Word is you and she were seeing each other and had a bad breakup."

Another chuckle, this time with a sardonic tinge. "In high school, maybe. Definitely not since." A long pause. "Listen, who is feeding you this stuff? I'd look to him. Or her. Sounds like somebody is trying to frame me. Adultery. Embezzling. Next thing you know, they'll try to say I stole your grandson and killed this journalist."

Carly drew a sharp breath at his words. She hadn't considered him a suspect in either case. Was this another case of implying guilt to have her disregard him as a suspect?

He broke into her thoughts. "Don't tell me you think that? I swear, I had nothing to do with Bradley's disappearance. I have grandkids of my own. I'd never hurt a child."

No, she didn't seriously consider him involved in that. But that didn't mean she'd stop looking at the books.

In her experience, a criminal often started with a single episode of law breaking, expanding into multiple times and numerous types out of desperation to cover the original crime. "I'll keep looking at the books. I'm pretty sure I can narrow the embezzlement down. Seems like it started about four months ago."

Four months. Four months. Why did that seem important? She was fairly certain she'd heard something about that recently.

But what?

And who?

$ $ $

After dinner, which Carly and Mike both picked at, they lingered over coffee. Silence reigned, allowing her time to rehash what she knew, what she conjectured, and how that all lined up with what others told her.

Leftover pasta and sauce cooled in their serving dishes on the table, and the last thing she wanted was to clean up.

Bradley was still missing. He could be out there alone. In the dark. Lost. Hurt. D—

She shook her head. She would not go there. He was fine. There was an innocent explanation.

There had to be.

Mike set his cup down. "Have you heard from Tom and Sarah?"

"Had an email saying they were trying to catch a flight back tonight and would get here as soon as they could."

She wasn't sure whether having them here would ease her mind, but she knew if it was her child missing, she'd be on scene.

"How about Denise and Don?"

"Thought I'd wait until tomorrow. It's a local news story, so I don't think the Riverdale media would cover it."

"Don't want them worrying if there's no need."

"I'll call later tonight. After the kids are gone to bed."

"Sounds good." He reached over and wrapped his hand around hers. "Now I know what you must have gone through when I went missing."

"Except then the police were saying you'd cleaned out our bank accounts and abandoned me."

He squeezed her fingers. "You never believed that."

She pursed her lips. "Oh, I don't know. There was maybe a minute when—"

"Really?"

"Really, no." She sighed. "I feel so useless just sitting here. Warm. Well-fed. With you."

"I know. But there's nothing you can do." He stared at a spot over her shoulder. "Do you think Bradley's disappearance could have anything to do with his father's shady past?"

"How do you mean?"

Sometimes Carly forgot that Bradley wasn't the natural son of Tom and Sarah. That he was the son of Mike's now-dead deadbeat brother Jerry.

"Just that he lived the first eight years of his life always moving, always running. No stability. No mother. Maybe he doesn't know how to settle down. Jerry never seemed to. Even when he was a kid, he always talked about running away."

"I didn't see that in Bradley."

Mike released her hand and clasped his on the table. "What if somebody from Jerry's past snatched him?"

"For what reason?"

"Ransom?"

"There'd be a call by now. Or a note. If they knew he was in town, they'd know he was staying with us."

"True. Revenge maybe?"

She stood and gathered plates and silverware. These dishes weren't going to march themselves to the dishwasher. "I can't go down that path. That's simply too evil to consider. And it gives me no hope of his safe return."

Mike picked up the pitcher of water and carried it to the fridge. "You're right. It can't be about that." He closed the door. "So what is it?"

"I don't know. But we will find him. Safe and sound. I won't rest until we do." She pushed him from the kitchen. "Now go back to work. I'll clean up, and then I have a call to make."

Almost as though her words conjured up the action, the phone rang. Mike snatched the receiver from the cradle. "Oh, hi. Yeah. That's great. See you soon."

Heart racing like a stampede of wildebeests, she leaned against the counter. "Who was it?"

"Tom and Sarah. They just landed in Portland and rented a car. They'll be here in about an hour."

"That's such good news." She surveyed the leftovers. "They'll probably be hungry. I can warm this up."

Having a plan always eased her mind.

Having a plan and a meal was almost heaven.

Knowing her kids were on the way left her mind free to work on other matters.

Next call: to Evie Mack.

And not a real surprise, but the mayor's secretary didn't sound too pleased to hear from her. "What do you want?"

"You saw the news?"

She harrumphed. "Me and everybody else. It's a lie."

"That was you and the mayor in the picture, wasn't it?"

"Right. And like I told that journalist guy, I don't know anything about it."

"The journalist?"

"Yeah. He came to my house this morning. Asking questions."

"What did you tell him?"

"Same thing I'm telling you. Mayor Akerman and I are not having, and have never had, a romantic relationship. He's my boss, for crying out loud."

Although not voiced, Carly heard the rest of that sentence: and old.

"Why would somebody stage this? Do you have any enemies?"

"I don't know what world you live in, Mrs. Turnquist. But I live a pretty quiet life. I go to work, I come home. I go to Augusta on the weekends to visit my fiancée. We plan our wedding. I don't cut people off in traffic. And when somebody else drives like a maniac, I don't give them the finger."

"How about the mayor? He have any enemies?"

"No." A pause. "Well, I don't think so. Of course, not everybody agrees with his politics. But they generally voice that in a town meeting, not by devising an elaborate smear campaign." The young woman sighed. "Now, if you don't mind, it's been a long and stressful day. Good night."

Dial tone buzzed through the line, and Carly replaced the handset. That was a waste of time. Except Evie confirmed the mayor's words.

Almost as if they colluded.

Had he called his secretary and coached her on what to say?

But why? Wouldn't the truth simply be easier?

Unless they didn't want her to know the truth.

$ $ $

An hour later, and Mike sat across the table from his son and daughter-in-law, wishing he could still tuck away the grub like he did when he was Tom's age.

Tom mopped up the last of the pasta sauce with a slice of bread while Sarah dished out ice cream all around, topping each with chocolate sauce and whipped cream. Conversation while eating was limited to asking for the salt or a bowl of food. House rules. And good rules they were.

But dessert—that was another matter.

Now they could get down to business.

When Sarah returned to the table with their sweet, Mike plowed right in, sharing the news about the photo of Bradley.

Sarah stirred her sauce and ice cream in her bowl. "So he made it to the park?"

Mike nodded. "And he didn't seem worried or afraid at that point. But there's no time stamp so we don't know for certain when that was."

Tom polished off the last spoonful. "What next?"

Mike exhaled. "Has Bradley been acting unusual lately?"

Sarah chuckled, the sweet melody releasing tension. "You mean for a nine-year-old boy?"

Carly pushed her empty bowl aside. "Boys are never usual. Or normal."

Mike gave his wife a sideways hug, happy her feisty attitude was returning. "You mistake their rambunctious behavior as a problem. Boys are naturally energetic."

Tom nodded. "And inquisitive."

Sarah pursed her lips then looked at her husband. "He was saying some weird stuff a week or so ago."

"Yeah. Right after that fight at school." Tom sat back in his chair. "I think the kids were teasing him, saying his father was a crook. And it got on his nerves. We had a talk, and he seemed fine after that."

A talk. A euphemism for many things, ranging from a simple discussion to an out-and-out argument. "What did he ask?"

Tom shrugged. "Wanted to know why kids were saying bad things about his father. That he lived a much more exciting life before. Traveling to great places. Staying in expensive hotels. Eating at the best restaurants."

Mike's brow drew down as he considered his son's words. "Doesn't sound like the life Jerry described to me. Down and out. Always one step ahead of the law and the mob. Getting beat up. Living in their car."

Tom sipped his coffee. "I didn't want to contradict him, but I did ask about the times that weren't exciting. When he was scared."

"And?"

"Didn't want to talk about that."

Carly shifted in her chair. "Do you think he might have run away? Trying to find that other life?"

Tom shook his head. "Don't think so. He seemed happy with us." He looked to Sarah. "What do you think?"

Her eyes glistened. "He's a scared little boy who lost his father, moved to a strange city, enrolled in a new school, and now has to fight off bullies who want to make his life miserable. How do you think he feels?"

Carly reached across the table and covered Sarah's hand with her own. "But he has a loving, stable home. Two parents who adore him. Grandparents who think the world of him."

Mike agreed, but another thought came to him. "Do you think it's possible somebody from his mother's family reached out to him? Asking Bradley to live with them?"

Tom's mouth turned down. "Possible, I guess, but unlikely. The adoption was closed because there was no known next of kin. Even if he wanted to go with his mother or her family, we had no way of finding them."

Sarah folded her arms across her chest. "Besides, his birth mother made her feelings quite clear when she abandoned him."

Just as Sarah was doing right now.

Interesting. He thought Carly was the only momma bear he knew.

His daughter-in-law just joined the don't-mess-with-my-kid club.

The doorbell rang, and Carly jumped up. "I'll get it."

There was no way Mike was sitting in the kitchen and waiting for news. He followed close behind.

For the second time that day, Chief Donovan stepped into their home, a file folder in one hand. "Got the coroner's report. Thought you might be interested."

Mike gestured to the living room. "I think you know the way."

Tom pulled a couple of chairs from the kitchen for him and his bride while the chief sniffed the air. "Smells like Italian."

Carly sat. "I'd offer you some, but a certain growing boy polished it off."

Donovan waved off her words. "No worries. I get off shift in another couple of hours. I'll have dinner then."

Mike smiled when his wife persevered with her interrogation of the lawman. "Oh, and will your wife cook your meal?"

"Not married. Haven't found the right woman, I guess."

Mike cleared his throat. "We don't want to keep you from your duties, Chief. Anything interesting in the report?"

The officer sat and opened the file. "The doc says Paulson was hit over the head with a blunt object, most likely the rock we found nearby. Preliminary tests confirm blood on the rock, but we're waiting for the lab to confirm whether it's the victim's. That finding actually makes it better for the killer."

Carly leaned forward. "No premeditation?"

"Right. Didn't bring the weapon. So no first-degree murder."

Carly sat back. "Could it have been robbery?"

"That's where the case takes a strange turn. See, up to this point, we figure he met somebody out there, they argued, and in the heat of passion, the killer struck out with the rock."

"Not robbery, then?"

Donovan faced Tom. "No. His wallet was in his pocket, along with a credit card and cash."

"Maybe he saw something—or somebody—he shouldn't have?"

The lawman turned to Mike. "Possibly. I don't think we'll know the motive until we find the killer."

"Which is going at it kind of backwards, isn't it?"

"Yes, Carly, it is. Not the best way, but we make do with what we have."

Mike peered at the chief. "You said the case takes a strange turn at this point."

"Right." He flipped through a couple of pages and took out a sheet of paper. "The picture in his hand. A publicity shot of the mayor. Looks like a newspaper image, perhaps."

Carly reached for the page. "Why would Paulson have this? It wasn't his photo, was it?"

"Nope. Near as we can tell, taken by another photographer at the local paper here in town."

Mike crossed one leg over the other. "So where does that leave us? And by us, I mean you."

"I think it gives me probable cause to get a search warrant on Mayor Akerman."

Carly sputtered. "You can't seriously think he killed the man, do you?"

"Possibly."

"Have you established a connection between them?"

"Not yet, but it's early days." The lawman stood and gathered back his photo. "Murder is serious business, but not as serious as finding Bradley. Until we do, this case is on the back burner. I've suggested the mayor not leave town, but—"

"But you can't legally detain him. Constructive detention, and all that."

Mike smiled at his wife. Sometimes she simply liked showing off.

The chief nodded. "Exactly. Good night."

He left, and once the door closed behind him, Carly returned to the kitchen and dug through the junk drawer.

Mike watched a few minutes. "What are you looking for?"

"A notepad."

"What for?"

"Duh. To make some notes."

Sarah stood and dragged Tom with her. "This is where Carly starts making lists and sorting out alibis and witnesses and motives and stuff. Let's clean up the kitchen."

Mike chuckled. "I'm out of here, too. Next thing you'll rope me into your investigation. And I won't be able to say no because I'll worry about you getting yourself into trouble and I'll feel like I have to help."

"Nothing wrong with working together."

"There is everything wrong with it. You're not a trained police investigator, and neither am I. We could go in and muck it all up."

"That's just one little thing, Mike. And I'll be careful. Promise."

He shook his head and left her to her list. No amount of talking or reminding her of other times when she was careful and still got into trouble would deter her.

She was bound and determined to plow on, full steam ahead.

The only thing he could do was make sure he was there to pick up the pieces when she got in over her head.

Which she always seemed to do.

Still, it was nice to be needed.

$$$

This was much better.

Bradley stretched out on the cot and pulled a blanket over him. His tummy was full. He wasn't thirsty anymore. A television played softly in the corner, and a light lit up the room.

Seemed like right after he thought about God, a woman came into the shed and took him by the hand. Then she led him across a yard, up some steps, and into a house. It was dark, so he couldn't see her face. Her hair looked dark, but not as dark as his mother's. A fence surrounded the yard so he couldn't see out. But he could see the stars overhead.

He tried to pull his hand from hers, but she yanked on his arm and held his hand tighter. When he pulled again, she smacked his bottom once, swift and hard, but there was no anger in her face.

She took him to the bathroom first, telling him to wash his hands when he was done, then she showed him the room where he now lay. A TV dinner waited for him on a desk, and one of his favorite shows featuring Spider Man, was just starting.

He wasn't as scared now as he was before.

But that didn't mean he was happy.

He still wanted to go home. Mommy and Daddy must be worried. Even way out in California, they would still get worried. He missed them. He missed Gramma Carly and Grampa Mike. And what about the eclipse? Would it still happen tonight? What would happen if he didn't get to take pictures? If he didn't see it, he couldn't write his report. His teacher wouldn't be able to give him a good grade.

He pushed the blanket back and got out of bed, creeping to the door. Maybe he should just go home. He rattled the door knob, but it wouldn't turn.

He was locked in.

Just like all those time in closets. And bathrooms. And even that one time in the car trunk. Locked in.

For his own good, his dad used to say.

But he didn't see how that could be right.

Wasn't it better for him to be with his mommy and daddy? Why would this man who grabbed him and this woman who locked him in this room want him? He wasn't anybody special. Maybe they wanted a little boy of their very own. Did that mean he'd never see his mommy and daddy again?

He crept back to bed and pulled the blanket over his head.

He wanted to go home.

Chapter 6

9:05 p.m.

Carly made her second call of the evening to the mayor, and judging by his deep exhale, he was none too thrilled to hear from her again.

But she would not be deterred.

"Just had a conversation with Chief Donovan."

Silence.

She waited a moment, then continued. "There are rumors floating around that you and Anita had a relationship. And a lot more recently than high school. Is it true?"

"Yes."

"Is it still going on?"

"No. I ended it about a year ago."

"So is it possible the baby is yours?"

"No."

Getting information from this man was like pulling teeth. "How can you be so sure?"

"My wife insisted I have the old snip-snip after we had our family."

Heat rose to her cheeks at the man's admission. "Why did the affair end?"

A chair squeaked from the other end of the call. "What does this have to do with the work I hired you to do?"

Nothing, honestly. She simply wanted to know. But she wouldn't tell him that. "I can't work for a man I can't trust. Plus, if you lie to me about one thing, how do I know you're not lying to me about the missing money? I have to explore all avenues."

"Good enough. I wanted to enter the political arena, and knew that public scrutiny could reveal the affair. So I ended it."

"Does your wife know?"

"Yes. I didn't want it coming back to bite me in the future."

"How did Anita take it?"

"How do you think? She wasn't happy, but she understood. Or she said she did."

A rabbit trail opened in front of her. "Did you take money from the town to pay off Anita so she wouldn't reveal your affair?"

Another sigh. "I had no need to. I never promised her anything more than a weekend here and there when my wife went out of town. That's all it ever was."

To him, perhaps. Affairs are rarely so cavalier for the woman. Despite what was said aloud. At least, according to supermarket tabloids.

"Did you ever meet with Harvey Paulson?"

The squeaking chair again. "No. But he called. Said he found something I'd want to see."

Now this was more like it. "Did he say what?"

"No. And I told him I wasn't interested in anything that couldn't be discussed over the phone. He said I had to see this to believe it."

"And?"

"He said he had one or two more things to check on and that maybe he'd just go to the source."

"Did he say who or what the source was?"

"I've told you everything that was said. He seemed like a crazy with an ax to grind, and I wasn't interested."

"With the picture leaked to the media, it seems as though somebody has it out for you. Any ideas who?"

Most people, in her experience, immediately jumped on that question, denying any reason for another person to seek revenge against them. And usually, they were correct. If there was a perceived threat, the basis was normally tenuous at best.

But Akerman didn't sputter and insist he lived a good, clean life, never beat his kids or kicked his dog.

Instead, another long silence filled the telephone line.

While she waited, Carly filed a couple of paid invoices and checked her bank balance online.

Finally he responded.

And not in the way she expected.

"Your allegations are starting to sound like a trash collection. In future, we will limit our discussions to the work you're doing to find the real criminal who stole the money. And don't call me at home again."

She stared at the handset for a while after he disconnected the call. It seemed the man did protest too much. He said his wife knew about the affair, but he didn't want her calling him at home.

Perhaps she shared a commonality with Mrs. Akerman—neither woman knew the whole story.

$$$

Across the office, Mike worked on his own little project: a flyer of Bradley. Seemed like for once he agreed with his wife. The police needed all the help they could get.

He lifted a stack of pages from the printer. Well, he was ready.

He glanced across the desk at his wife who stared at the handset buzzing in her hand. "Uh, Carly, that's the second time tonight he hung up on you. And based on what I heard of the conversation, I'd probably do the same thing."

"I needed to know the answers to those questions. And he wasn't exactly forthcoming."

"Correction. You wanted to know the answers. You aren't the police. And you can't go around acting like you are. Can you imagine the haranguing he'll give Donovan when the chief asks him the same questions? He might even tell the man he already spoke to you. Do you think that will make the police chief happy?"

"If he's not happy, it's not my fault. He should have already asked Akerman about the rumors of him and Anita. And the baby. I mean, the motive is as clear as the nose on his face. And Paulson was clutching the picture of the mayor in his hand."

He tapped the flyers into an orderly bundle. "Want to go for a walk?"

"How can you even think of exercise at a time like this? Our grandson is missing, a murderer stalks the streets of our small town, and the town is out tens of thousands of dollars. I don't even know the amount yet for certain. And you want to go out, risk your life, and raise your heart rate. For what?"

He handed a page to her. "Thought we could hand these out, talk to people. See who's around town. See who looks guilty."

"Oh."

He knew his wife almost better than she knew herself.

He had her at the word 'guilty'.

He stood and offered his arm. "Tom and Sarah could probably use a distraction, too. And since they're on west coast time, they should be wide awake."

Carly planted a kiss on his cheek. "You are so smart."

"And handsome."

"That too." She slipped her arm through his. "Lead on."

Within a few minutes, the four headed on foot for downtown. As they neared Main Street, voices and lights indicated the presence of more people than claimed the town as home.

Sidewalks on both sides of the street were jammed with people, vendor carts hawking everything from hot dogs to viewing glasses—which any idiot should know weren't needed but still boasted a strong business—to t-shirts to postcards.

Seemed anybody and everybody with something even remotely connected to the eclipse was in town, selling their wares.

Mike paused at the corner. "How about we split into couples and cover both sides of the street?"

Tom nodded and held out his hand for flyers. "Sounds good. We can meet up at the entrance to the park and go from there."

Mike and Carly continued down the harbor side of the street, stopping to talk with the few townsfolk out and about that evening, although most of the revelers were strangers. Seemed residents decided to stay home.

They were probably smart.

And if he wasn't looking for his grandson, Mike would do the same.

Just past the pharmacy, he spotted Chief Donovan. He quirked his chin in the direction of the lawman who leaned against his police cruiser, arms folded over his chest, looking every bit the grim authority. "Do you want to stop and chat?"

"I think not. Let's keep going."

The chief nodded in their direction as they passed but didn't speak. Mike exhaled when they were out of earshot, fully expecting to feel the strong hand of the law clamped on his shoulder.

At the next corner, they paused. Mike gazed across the harbor. The water beat a steady rhythm against the shore, and boats bobbed lazily on the surface. Several he didn't recognize confirmed out-of-towners taking advantage of the clear sky to observe the moon do what it had done for thousands of years. Or more. Depending on a person's belief about the age of things.

He looked up again into the inky sky dotted with stars and planets. Tears blurred his vision as he thought of Bradley. Out there.

Perhaps alone. Maybe looking up at the same moon and stars right now. Was he scared? Was he hurt?

A lump in his throat threatened to choke him, and he wished at that moment, as he had on a few other occasions, that he believed in Someone bigger that he could lean on for help. For peace. For answers.

His daughter seemed to have that. And his son-in-law and granddaughter. Most of the time he didn't give their faith a second thought.

But tonight—tonight he envied them.

He took Carly's arm and headed for the park, pushing past throngs of people in town for a good time. Here he was, out on a serious venture, trying to find Bradley, while—as Carly said—a murderer roamed the streets and a little boy struggled to get back home. It was enough to make a body angry.

Kind of the same way he felt when Sophie, his first wife, died. Everybody around him went on with their lives. Even his friends and family. After the funeral, it was like he was expected to simply move on. To forget her. To not notice that they were laughing and living and loving while she wasn't. At the time, it didn't seem fair. At the time, it made him angry.

Just like now.

But it wasn't these strangers' fault. Which is the same conclusion he came to all those years ago. He had children to raise. A business to run. A household to maintain. He had no time—or energy—to spend pondering why otherwise everything seemed so wrong.

A group of three revelers, intoxicated or high, based on their weaving steps and high-pitched laughter, blocked the walkway. He pulled Carly closer and stepped to the side as they went past, one of them leering into his face. His free hand clenched into a fist, ready to protect his wife if need be, but when his eyes locked with the man— no, a boy, really—the boy backed off and apologized.

Mike shook himself. He was ready to clock that kid simply because they were having a good time and he wasn't. He needed to check his attitude. He wouldn't be any good to Bradley—or himself or his family—if he let anger get in the way.

At the entrance to the park, they waited a few minutes until Tom and Sarah arrived. Between them, they had about twenty of the original one hundred flyers left.

Mike led the way to a low rock wall where they sat. "Anything to report?"

Sarah shook her head. "Most everybody we talked to—when we could find someone sober enough to make sense—said they came into town late this afternoon and didn't recall seeing a boy by himself."

Tom nodded. "We had one possible who said she saw him walk past her shop that morning. But we already knew that."

Sarah released the scrunchie holding back her hair, raked her fingers through her tresses, and refastened it. "We did talk to a few businesses that were still open, and they posted the flyer in their window."

Mike kicked himself mentally. They should have thought of that. Then again, they saw Mrs. Olson, and she was just locking up. Town hall was closed, and the police and fire stations already had his picture out. "Do we walk the park and talk to people?"

Tom reached out a hand. "How about you give us the flyers and we'll keep going while you guys head home? You already looked in the park today. Maybe a fresh set of eyes?"

Carly gripped his arm, and Mike already knew what she wanted. She would stay out here looking until she dropped, if she had her way.

But an exhausted Carly was of no use to anybody. And she still had a murderer to find. Unofficially, of course. Not that he could get that through to her. The unofficial part.

He looped an arm over her shoulder. "We'll head home. I'll keep a couple of flyers to hand out to any shops still open. And we'll call Denise and let her know what's going on."

Tom grinned. "Sounds like a plan. See you at home."

Mike linked hands with his wife, and, although she resisted for a moment, soon they retraced their steps back along Main Street. The pharmacy was dark, but Mike tucked a flyer through the mail slot. The kind old woman would surely hang it in the window in the morning.

Although, by that time, any witness who might lead them to Bradley could be gone.

$$$

Carly sank into her favorite chair at home, all strength sapped from her. In fact, all she wanted to do was go to bed, pull the covers over her head, and wake up tomorrow with Bradley safe in his room. Discovering all this was a bad dream.

But she didn't need to pinch herself to know she was fully awake.

And her grandson was still missing.

And a stranger to the town was still dead.

Were the two connected?

It seemed unlikely that they weren't. And yet what link could exist between a second-rate newspaper hack and her grandson? Apart from the fact they met at the bus station just over twenty-four hours before. Nothing that she could come up with.

And was the eclipse a cover for a crime? Or merely coincidence?

She would get to the bottom of this, and somebody would pay for the worry and time lost and—well, for everything. She'd see to that.

Right now, though, she needed to call Denise and let her know what was going on. She dialed the number. "Hi, Denise, how are you?"

"Doing okay, Carly. So good to hear your voice."

"Did you watch the news today?"

"No, we just got back from an overnight sleepover slash camping trip with Margie and her class. They went to a Boy Scout campground up Bangor way. We had fun and fed the mosquitoes. Why, what's up?"

An ache filled the back of Carly's throat as she tried to explain. "Bradley came to spend a couple of days while Tom and Sarah were out of town. To see the eclipse. Not Tom and Sarah, of course. Bradley. He came here to see the eclipse. And now they're here. And he's not." She stifled a sob that came out as a hiccup. "Oh, I'm not making any sense."

"Are you telling me Bradley is missing?"

"Yes."

"In Bear Cove?"

"Yes." Guilt over her failure to keep her grandson safe wore a hole in her heart. "And it's all my fault."

"Is that what Tom and Sarah said?"

"No, of course not. They'd never say that. They've been absolutely wonderful. They're out walking in the park right now. We just came back from handing out flyers downtown and talking to people."

"What do the police say?"

Carly exhaled. "Oh, you know. The standard thing. Following all leads. Doing everything possible." She swiped at her tears. "I feel so useless."

"What else is going on?"

"What makes you think there is something else going on?"

Denise chuckled. "Because you're involved. There's always something else going on."

"You did hear the news, then?"

"We caught the tail end of the regional news on the way home. Nothing was mentioned about Bradley, although if they didn't mention his name, I would never think it was him missing, since I didn't expect him to be there. No, they did say an investigation was under way into the murder of a journalist. No leads. No persons of interest at this time. Blah, blah, blah."

"Harvey Paulson. He was in town to cover the eclipse."

"Doesn't seem like a reason to be killed. It's not like he had a scoop on it, or something."

A scoop. Harvey talked about getting the scoop on a story. But the news about the mayor didn't break until today. After he was already dead. So that couldn't be the story he was looking into.

Unless he was the one who leaked that picture? Or doctored it, depending on who she really believed, the news story or the mayor.

"Right. But he came here the day he died and wanted to talk to me. And I sent him away."

"That's not like you."

"It was late, and I thought he was a creep. Now I wish I hadn't."

"Of course. He might have been able to tell you why someone would want him dead."

"Well, I didn't know that at the time, did I? That he would die."

"No. And apparently, neither did he."

"I just wanted to let you know about Bradley so if you saw it on the news, you wouldn't be worried."

Denise chuckled again, the gentle sound easing the ache in Carly's head. "Knowledge isn't what gives peace. Only God can do that. Can I pray for you and for Tom and Sarah and Dad? You must all be worried sick."

"You know your dad. He doesn't say much about his feelings. And your brother is cut from the same cloth. You know where I stand about your faith. But if it makes you feel better, go ahead."

"Heavenly Father, Abba Daddy, You know how much we love Bradley. You have a Son so You know how we feel. We're worried about him. And we know You have him in Your hands. So please, God, please give us peace to let You do Your work in this situation. In our lives. Show us what to do. And make it clear when we're to sit back and let You do what You do best—bring Your lost children home. In Jesus' name, Amen."

Her daughter-in-love's words touched a place deep in her heart, and she pondered them.

Bring your lost children home.

Bradley was lost.

And in some ways, she felt lost, too. Unable to count on her own abilities or training or experience to solve the mystery of his disappearance. What if they never found him? What if somebody had grabbed him and taken him away forever? Maybe for revenge. Maybe because they wanted a son of their own. Maybe for other more sinister reasons.

Would Denise's God be able to give her peace then?

If He could, He could bring Bradley home. Right now. So why didn't He?

If He couldn't, if He wasn't big enough to solve her problems, then He wasn't big enough to have any place in her life.

Maybe God was just another mystery to add to her list.

$$$

Bradley peered out the window in the small room he now occupied. The sun was down and the sky was dark, but the stars shone like little lights. The nursery rhyme from when he was a kid filled his head.

Twinkle, twinkle, little star. How I wonder what you are.

His teacher said the sun was a star, but that didn't seem right. She said it was so bright because it was so close to the earth. Well, he didn't know about that, but it sure seemed weird that all the other stars were so tiny. Because they were so far away, she said.

Far away. That's how Mommy and Daddy and Grampa Mike and Gramma Carly felt right now. So far away, he couldn't see them.

He cupped his hands around his eyes and pretended he was looking through his telescope. Not a real expensive one, not like a real astronomer would use, but still powerful enough to see the marks on the moon surface, he liked his telescope. And with the night vision scope, he could see tiny pinpricks of light in the dark sky.

He crooked his neck and peered up. Couldn't see the moon yet. Would he miss the whole thing?

He sighed and stepped away from the window. A half-eaten bag of chips, a couple of sodas, and a chocolate bar waited for him on the table beside the bed. But his tummy rumbled, and he wished he had an apple. Or a bowl of cereal. Maybe he'd ask the lady who looked after him if he could have something else to eat. Junk food sounded fun, but it wasn't. Just thinking about eating the bar made his teeth ache.

A toothbrush. He'd ask for one. The lady seemed nice. Sometimes he heard other voices, mostly women, but a couple of times, a man. But she warned him not to call out. And when he heard the man, that scared him, and so he stayed quiet, hiding under the blanket.

He looked back then returned to the window and placed his hands flat against the glass. Still no moon. Were Mommy and Daddy looking at the sky right now? Wondering where he was? He stood moon. Maybe Mommy and Daddy could feel him thinking about them. Isn't that what Margie said one time? That God always knows where he is and what he's doing. He thought that was kind of strange, but then Mommy said she knew he took that last cookie because she has eyes in the back of her head. So maybe God is like that, too.

Well, if God was anything like Mommy and Daddy, that would be good.

Knowing that somebody who loved him knew where he was seemed important.

Thursday, October 28th

Chapter 7

1:15 a.m.

An emptiness invaded Carly's heart and home. Without Bradley, the eclipse seemed a non-event. At least for her.

And, too, it seemed, for his parents, and for Mike.

The next morning, the blaring of horns drew her to walk to the corner of Old Tom's Hill and Main. A long line of cars stretched as far as the eye could see, heading out of town. Clusters of people strolled Main Street, mostly congregating around the Dew Drop Inn, where a line formed for patrons awaiting a table inside.

With the others still abed—who knew there was a seven o'clock in the morning?—she decided to roam a little. Work out the cobwebs caused by a restless night of waking frequently to worry about her grandson.

Up ahead, a small knot of women clustered on the sidewalk, bent over something that attracted their attention. Carly paused and studied their curious behavior. An injured kitten? A stunned bird?

The group parted, revealing their focus.

Bradley!

No, her mind played tricks on her. Wishing and wanting and praying made her see things that weren't there.

But his eyes locked with hers. Eyes so much like Mike's.

She trotted toward him, his name on her lips, but unable to draw a deep enough breath to utter the word, for fear of breaking the spell—or whatever it was—that conjured him here.

He brushed off the hands of strangers reaching for him, and raced to her like something out of a sappy card commercial. Slow motion never seemed so slow and distance never seemed so far.

But when he launched himself into her embrace, and the solidity of his body pressed against her, the strength of his arms around her waist, the smell of the outdoors clinging to his hair, she knew he was no illusion.

Her grandson was home again.

And she never wanted this moment to end.

Margaret from the Snip 'n Clip joined them. "He walked up to us like he didn't know where he was. We thought maybe he was hurt."

Carly tipped his face up. "Are you okay?"

He nodded, dark circles smudging the skin beneath his eyes. "I'm hungry. And cold."

The stylist patted his head, and he shied away from her touch.

Had somebody hit him?

Her fists and her jaw clenched. If anybody—

He squeezed her hand. "Can we go home now?"

Home. The sweetest word he could utter.

She gathered him into her arms again then released him and gripped his hand. "Yes, absolutely. There's somebody there who'll be glad to see you."

When they entered the house, the rest of the household was up. Voices, the coffeemaker's burble, and Doc's meowing testified to the fact that the kitchen was the hub of activity.

Carly put her finger across her lips. "Let's sneak in and surprise them."

Bradley nodded. "I hear Mommy's voice. And Daddy's."

"They've been very worried about you."

His serious expression made him look very grown up. "I've been worried about them, too."

She allowed him to take the lead, following close behind, unwilling to let him out of her sight. At least not until he turned twenty-one. Which could prove challenging when he returned home to New York with his parents.

But for right now, she had him safe in sight.

Bradley stepped around the corner, out of sight. Sarah squealed and dropped a plate. A chair pushed back from the table and tipped over. Doc screeched as though his tail was stepped on. And Mike's stifled sob tore at Carly's heart.

She peeked around the corner. Her family was reunited.

After much hugging and crying and more hugs and pats on the head and questions and shrugging—most of the latter from Bradley—they settled at the table. Carly had so many questions to ask, but she deferred to his parents.

Unless, of course, they didn't ask the right ones.

Eventually they worked out of him that he made it to the park, but then his smile fell away.

Carly couldn't stand it any longer. "Did you meet the man from the bus station again?"

He nodded. "He asked me if I remembered us talking about a scoop. Of course I did. He said he had the biggest scoop of all. One that would make his career."

She laid a hand on his arm. "Did he say what it was?"

"No. But he had a picture in his hand. He took it out of his pocket after he took my picture. He promised to send me the picture he took of me."

"When was this?"

A shrug. "After I went for a walk. Then he said he had an important meeting. Right there in the park. I told him about a bench I saw, and he laughed. Said it wasn't that kind of a meeting. This one called for dis—dis—discre—"

His mother leaned forward. "Discretion?"

He nodded. "Yeah. That word. I didn't know what it meant, but I didn't want to look dumb, so I nodded and left. Found a really good place to set up my telescope and camera. On top of the hill." His smile fell away. "But on the way home, I got lost. Went down the wrong street. And I saw a man coming out of a house. He chased me."

Tom put an arm over his son's shoulders. "Why would he do that?"

Another shrug. "Dunno. He came out, kissed a lady holding a baby, turned around and saw me and chased me." Tears filled his eyes. "I couldn't run fast because of my stuff, and I thought maybe he wanted to steal my camera or something, so I didn't want to just drop it."

Sarah swiped at a tear that trickled down his cheek. "Take your time."

Bradley drew a couple of deep breaths then cleared his throat. "I ran into the woods, but I kept tripping on the roots and rocks. I fell a couple of times. The he caught me. I thought he might push me to the ground and take my stuff, but he didn't. He grabbed me by the shoulder. Told me to be quiet."

Tom refilled his orange juice. "Would you know the house again?"

The boy's mouth turned down. "Maybe. I mean, all the houses look the same. I think it was white with blue trim."

Great. That narrowed it down to about half the town.

Carly wriggled in her chair. "Then what?"

"He took me back to her house."

Mike wrapped his hands around his cup. "Her house?"

The boy nodded. "The lady with the baby."

Tom laid a hand on his son's arm. "How did you get away?"

"I was looking out the window of the room she put me in."

Sarah hugged him close. "They kept you in a house?"

He nodded. "First I was in a shed. Then they brought me inside. I could hear ladies talking. And sometimes a baby cried. But I stayed real quiet, because she said if I made a noise, the man would hurt me. I watched TV, and I ate chips and stuff." He rubbed his stomach. "I'd really like to have some vegetables, please."

His father chuckled. "Well, that's first. We usually have to bribe you to eat anything green."

Bradley turned solemn eyes on them. "I got tired of chips and chocolate."

Carly stood. "I'll put some broccoli in the steamer while you keep telling us your story."

She retrieved the green veg from the crisper in the refrigerator and trimmed the ends before setting it to cook. Then she returned to the table just as her grandson finished his tale.

"I tried to figure out what to do. The lady was nice, but she was real careful. She kept the door locked when she wasn't there, and when she came in, she locked it with a key she kept in her pocket." He pumped his arms like a bodybuilder. "I wanted to be all grown up and strong so I could push her out of the way, but I wasn't. So I used a knife the lady left on my tray by mistake to loosen the screw that held the window shut. I cut out the screen and climbed out. Then I ran until I got to the street."

Mike piped up. "How did you know which way to go?"

"I didn't, really. But I knew the park should be behind me, and the harbor was on this side." He held up his right hand. "And I saw lots of cars and people. So I ran that way."

Sarah pulled him close again, and this time, instead of squirming as most nine-year-old boys would, he rested in her arms. "You are so brave. And so smart."

Carly considered his words. Anita? There could be any number of women with babies living in town. Even living in the houses near the park.

Then who was the man? Bob Whalen? Or somebody else?

But a better question was why would an upstanding member of their community kidnap a young boy? Did it have to do with what Bradley saw? Sure, Bob was married, but Bradley had no idea it wasn't his wife. And once the boy left town, any danger of an affair being revealed would go with him.

No, there had to be another reason.

Perhaps it didn't have anything to do with who he was with.

But that he was near the woods.

Close to the spot where the journalist's body was found.

She needed to check alibis.

$$$

Two hours later, Bradley rested in his bed, with Tom and Sarah guarding from the living room. Carly had already called the chief and let him know the boy was home safe and sound. She downplayed his disappearance, wanting to look into the matter herself first. If the police got onto Bob and Anita, she wouldn't get within a mile of them.

They would eventually answer to the law, but right now, they'd answer to her.

She called Anita, brushing aside the woman's breezy greeting and biting back the accusations she wanted to fling like mud pies. "I'll cut right to the reason for the call. Your baby. The mayor isn't the father, is he?"

"No. But I never said he was. Somebody has been spreading vicious lies."

"Is Bob Whalen the father?"

"My personal life is none of your business."

It was when it concerned her grandson, but Carly wouldn't let that piece of valuable information loose just yet. She didn't have any proof yet that Bob and Anita were behind Bradley's experience. Plus, she had another reason to question the woman's thought processes and decision-making skills. "You're on the town council. You make important financial decisions for our town. You have access to the bank account. And money is missing."

"I didn't take it."

Interesting turn of phrase. She didn't say she didn't know anything about it. Simply that she didn't take it.

"What is your relationship with Bob Whalen?"

"Again, none of your business. And he's a married man. We could both sue you for libel. Or slander. Whichever it is."

"I'm not making any accusations. Simply trying to find the truth."

"Your truth, maybe. And you won't find it here. We're done."

The line went dead.

She shrugged. Oh, well. On to the next unpleasant item on her list. But this one needed doing in person.

When he answered the door, Bob glanced past her as though expecting to see somebody else.

Who? Anita? Maybe the cops?

"Hi, Bob. Got a minute?"

"Well, I was in the middle of something." Despite his characterization of the mayor, Bob employed his own used-car-salesman's banter. He hesitated then stepped back. "But sure. I guess I can spare a few minutes."

She stepped inside. "Good. I won't take up much of your valuable time."

The inside of his home was cool and dim, mostly due to the drawn blinds. The furniture in the living room was older and well-worn, and toys scattered on the floor confirmed he was a family man making ends meet. Which seemed a little odd, given that his wife was loaded. With money. Then again, perhaps her tight-fistedness wasn't only legendary, but real, as well.

He stood just inside the foyer, arms across his chest. "Hey, Carly. How's things going in the bean counting world?"

She gritted her teeth. The man should talk to her husband. Mike would confirm she was anything but boring, contrary to popular opinion. "Haven't counted beans in a month or so, Bob, but thanks for asking."

"What can I do for you today? Still looking under rocks for something slimy to wriggle past?"

Good. Already on the defensive. Right where she wanted him. And for some reason, he didn't want her seeing the rest of his home. "Just talked to Anita."

"Oh?" Gone were both the banter and the aggressive tone of his previous comment. "What did she say?"

If he'd come right out and added "that she shouldn't have said", his message couldn't have been more clear.

As she suspected, these two had something to hide.

What, she wasn't certain.

But she would ferret it out of him.

She took another step into the living room. "How's your wife and kids?"

He stiffened. "What about them?"

"Just asking. Trying to be neighborly."

He crossed his arms over his chest. "Look. We're not friends. Probably won't be, so let's cut the goody two shoes act."

From somewhere in the rear of the house, a bell tinkled.

She glanced in that direction. "Lunch ready? I'm starved."

He looked down the hallway. "Not food. My negatives are finished processing."

"Negatives?"

"Yes. I have a small dark room. I'm an amateur photographer."

Another interesting tidbit. "How nice. What are your favorite subjects?"

He pointed to a gallery of images on one wall of the living room. "My family."

"Oh. So you like taking pictures of people. I've been thinking of getting our family portrait—"

"No."

She stared at him. How rude. "I'd be happy to pay."

"I only take pictures of family."

"Oh. Anything else?"

One shoulder lifted and fell. "Birds. Waves. Boats."

She chuckled. "Well, living in Bear Cove, there's definitely lots of that." She turned toward the door. "If you change your mind about that family portrait thing—"

"I won't."

She whirled around, feeling like she was being given the bum's rush. "But if you ever do—"

"Goodbye, Carly."

"If I have other questions—"

"Perhaps I should have my attorney present. This feels like harassment."

"Not at all, Bob. Just trying to get answers to questions that impact the scope of my work for the town. Catching criminals and all that, you know."

The man's face paled, as though he'd seen a ghost.

Or just realized she was serious in her quest to reveal the embezzler.

But if he was innocent, why should that be so worrisome to him?

$$$

Funny, Mike's car wasn't in the driveway when she returned home. Tom and Sarah's rental sat forlornly by itself. Carly pulled through into the garage. Maybe he ran out to grab some milk or bread. And if what she stocked the fridge with was gone, that was a good sign. Meant Bradley's appetite returned.

She stepped into the foyer and living room. Tom and Sarah snoozed on the sofa, and Mike's reading glasses lay on the coffee table. She hung up her keys and set her purse on the floor.

Doc, the cat, uncurled himself from Sarah's feet and wound around her ankles. "Nobody feed you today? Come with me."

The marmalade feline bounded toward the kitchen, and she opened the fridge to snag the can of cat food.

Which sat beside a full gallon of milk and three-quarters of a loaf of bread.

So what took Mike out?

She spooned food into the cat's bowl then headed for the living room. Tom opened one eye. "Where's your dad?"

A huge yawn, displaying all his molars. "Said that since things were under control here, he'd head up to the home improvement store on the highway to pick up a couple of locks."

"Locks? What for?"

Tom shrugged. "Something about making sure the house and everybody in it is safe."

She sighed. "Bradley didn't go missing from the house."

"I tried to use that logic, too, but he wasn't listening. Had it in his head we needed more locks. Here, and in New York. Even mentioned something about getting some for Denise."

"How long has he been gone?"

"Dunno. I was only half awake."

The landline phone rang, and Carly picked up the receiver. "Mike, we don't need any more locks."

Chief Donovan's voice filled the line where she expected her husband's. "Sorry, Carly. Not Mike."

"What's new, Chief?"

"Got bad news, I'm afraid."

She sank to the arm of her chair. "What is it?"

"Mike's been in a bad accident. Up near the highway. In fact, the road is still closed. Likely will be until late tomorrow.”

Her world turned black around the edges. She closed her eyes. This couldn’t be happening. He just went up to the highway. “How bad?”

“Too soon to say. He’s on his way to the community hospital. They’ll assess him there, make the decision if he needs to be airlifted to Riverdale. Or Augusta. Hospital suggested you call before you go there, in case they sent him on.”

“I’ll do that.”

“There’s something else, Carly.”

There was always one more thing. But how bad could it be?

“The car—and Mike, too—reeked of alcohol. I’ve ordered a felony blood test. Looks like he was drunk as a skunk.”

This was bad.

Real bad.

“You must be wrong, Chief. Mike was sober as a priest when I saw him less than an hour ago. And Tom never said anything about his dad drinking before he left to go out.”

“All I know is what Bob told me.”

Her heart sank. “Bob?”

“Yeah, Bob Whalen. He was driving by. Saw Mike slumped over the wheel. He’s a paramedic, you know.”

“Right. I just saw—” Oops, better not let on that she was just at Bob’s house asking questions even remotely connected to the murder. “I mean, I know.”

“Yeah, well, he saw the accident. Checked on Mike. Called the ambulance and stayed with him until it arrived and they transported him. Lucky thing, too. He had quite the gash on his forehead, apparently. Difficulty remembering. Talking. The whole bit.”

“Thanks, Chief.”

She hung up. Strange. When she left Bob’s house—just minutes before this accident—he was up to his elbows in his dark room. He hadn’t told her anything about going out. Which, of course, he might not. He wasn’t exactly thrilled with her visit or her questions.

In fact, the only time he did seem pleased was when she said she was leaving.

But the timing of his arrival at the accident scene—if that’s what it really was—appeared a little too coincidental to her.

Serendipity, almost.

Chapter 8

Carly waited while her call was transferred for the third time. Bradley sat in Mike's office chair, chin cupped in his hands, elbows resting on the desk. She tossed him a smile as the line clicked, indicating a human on the other end. "Hi, it's Carly Turnquist. Wanted to check on my husband Mike. The police told me he was brought in from a car accident?"

"Yes. He's in surgery now."

"How long before I can talk to him?"

"Let me check the notes." Papers rustled. "Looks like a laceration on his forehead that the ER doc felt was best addressed through surgery rather than just stitches. Might need plastic surgery later on, so he wanted to do a tidy job. A couple of bruised ribs. Let me see. Hmm."

Carly hated when a medical person made that unique sound that usually came out resembling an unvoiced question wrapped in a suppressed exclamation buried in a reprimand.

It was never good news.

"Small bleeder in the abdomen according to the MRI that he wanted to check out, too."

"When can I see him?"

"He should be in surgery at least another hour, then perhaps another hour until he returns to his room. He's listed as stable, which was upgraded once he was examined, so that's good news. Save your energy and wait a couple of hours."

Carly thanked the nurse and hung up.

Save her energy indeed.

Not.

She needed to go out. But Tom and Sarah were gone—heading for the hospital despite the chief's suggestion to call first. "I guess you're with me."

Bradley shrugged. "That's okay. I don't mind."

She ruffled his hair. Since when did getting stuck with Gramma become such a sacrifice? She held out her hand. "Want to go out?"

"Maybe we can find my stuff."

Right. She'd completely forgotten about his missing stuff. No doubt wherever they found it would be the place he was kept.

"Maybe we can. But first, I have to make two more phone calls. Quick ones."

He sighed and settled back into the chair, looking so much like Mike that her heart ached to have her husband home again safe and sound. She called Denise to let her know about her father's accident, assuring her she'd call as soon as she had an update, promising to get Mike to call her when he could talk. A voice message left on Tom's phone promised to look after Bradley, although the words stung. She hadn't done such a good job before, had she?

Then she and Bradley left the house in her car. First they'd check out the scene of the accident, then she planned to drive through the couple of side streets off Main. Perhaps Bradley would recognize the house where he saw the man and woman kiss, and where the man ultimately grabbed him.

Despite being the day after the eclipse, traffic was heavy on Main and parking spots were full. She inched her car forward, ignoring the driver on her right who wanted to merge in ahead of her. She had an important mission, and he was a tourist with plenty of time on his hands.

Besides, she had a date at the hospital in—she checked the clock on the dash—an hour and forty minutes. Mr. Tourist could wait another minute or so.

Up ahead, a car did a u-turn and came back, heading in the other direction. Within minutes, the vehicles in front of her did the same. Horns blared, and the scowls on the faces of the drivers indicated something ahead caused their displeasure. She forged ahead. Until she came to a barrier across the road declaring the road was closed.

She exhaled. Apparently the chief was right when he told her the same thing. Not that she doubted him. Really. The police could have concluded their accident investigation or reconstruction or whatever they called it and opened the road.

Then again, if Bob and Anita weren't guilty of anything except poor choices in bed mates, the closed road would keep other suspects in town.

Not that she wanted—or needed—her pool of possibly guilty people increased.

No wonder the other drivers were unhappy.

A car parked at the curb backed up, and she gave the driver the space he needed to get onto the road and turn around, then she promptly pulled in. Putting the car in park and turning off the engine, she turned to her grandson. "Up for a short walk?"

He grinned, the freckles on the bridge of his nose disappearing into the crinkles. "Sure. Are we gonna find my stuff?"

"Maybe."

Honestly, she didn't know what they'd find. Something important, she hoped. Something to vindicate her husband, she fervently prayed.

As they walked, she thought back to Denise's reaction to her call. Concern. Worry. And then peace. Quick as a flash. Before she even heard that her father was upgraded to stable. Unlike Carly, whose heart raced, pounded, and fluttered—all at the same time. The mere suggestion she might lose Mike panicked her.

But not Denise. Who then offered to pray *with* her and *for* her. The idea she even needed prayer hadn't crossed her own mind.

Whatever this peace was, Carly wanted a good dose of it.

And although she wasn't certain she could attribute her current clarity of thinking and rationality of reasoning to the prayer, she was glad she had it.

She'd have to give this more thought.

When she had time. When she had nothing else on her mind. Not trying to reveal a murderer. Or find a kidnapper. Or prove her husband innocent of drunk driving.

When life got back to normal.

Whenever that was.

She'd like to live in Normal, even for a long weekend.

About a quarter of a mile outside town, she found the spot she looked for. Police crime scene tape fluttered in the breeze. A dark stain like oil pooled on the gravel shoulder. A guard rail looking the worse for wear and bearing scrapes of paint the color of Mike's vehicle—a red SUV—bore testament to the accident. Fragments of orange lens covers and shards of auto glass littered the ground.

"I think this is it."

Bradley kept a grip on her hand, which was fine with her. Easier to keep him from messing up the scene that way. Although the myriad of police, paramedic, and technician boots had already done that. She sighed. Once they made up their mind about the cause and circumstances, they did little to preserve evidence that might prove otherwise. Although, to give them credit, most of the time they were correct.

But not this time. Mike did not drink and drive. He rarely consumed alcohol, and he had too much at stake to be foolish. Even for something as important to him as the safety of his family.

So what really happened? Apparently Bob subscribed to the initial story of drunk driving. How had he gotten here so quickly? Maybe there was a simple explanation. He realized he was low on a chemical or a supply, so he headed out to—to where? There was nothing on this road except trees and rocks. Up on the highway, the home improvement store. A liquor store. The twenty-four-hour photo lab she was supposed to take Bradley's pictures to and had completely spaced out. And a major retailer.

Not likely he could buy photographic supplies at any of those businesses.

But he could buy alcohol.

No, that was too ludicrous to even consider. Why would anybody—particularly Bob, who barely knew Mike—want to tarnish a man's good name and reputation by staging an accident and setting him up as a criminal? Had Mike ticked somebody off recently? She searched her memory. Nothing jumped out at her. It had been months since the fiasco of his murdered client where he was framed when he disappeared. Unlikely this was connected.

Maybe somebody was hoping he'd go completely off the road and die. Except the guardrail stopped the car. Again, why?

She moved to the edge of the shoulder furthest from the road and peered over. Thick trees posed a deadly barricade, accented with boulders the size of a small car. Had he gone over, most likely he would have died.

She shivered. So close.

A flicker of color caught her attention. Something red down there. She glanced at Bradley. "Stay here."

But the boy wouldn't release his grip on her hand. She twisted and turned her fingers, trying to disengage from his hold. Finally, she gave up. "Okay. But be careful. We're going down there."

Together they slipped and slid down over the steep bank toward her target, which turned out to be a makeshift tent made of a blanket held up by a rope tied between two trees. Patches indicated it was an old blanket. Perhaps a long-term encampment. Cantaloupe-sized rocks pinned down the corners, and a small fire pit—now cold— suggested the camp was more than simply overnight.

She hesitated at the bottom of the incline, her grandson close beside her. No telling what kind of person—or people—lived here. Called this crude abode their home—even temporarily.

A man emerged from the shelter. His bushy beard and unkempt hair, both grizzled and unruly, baggy pants, and dirty hands and face indicated his rough lifestyle and advancing age. Hanging from a tree, a sack that dangled in the breeze. Food, perhaps?

She pasted on a smile but refrained from offering her hand. No telling what a man like this might do if given the opportunity to grab her and pull her into his tent. "Hi."

The man stopped and studied them. "Hello."

His tone bespoke education, his accent regional, his tentative smile non-aggressive.

She exhaled. "I was wondering if you saw the accident up there earlier today?" She quirked her chin up the bank. "A red car?"

"Station wagon-like thing?"

Things were looking up. "Yes. An SUV. Driven by a man."

"Ran into the guardrail. Thought it might come on over." He pointed to a tree with a blackened scorch pattern near its base. "The last one did."

"Last one?"

"Car accident. About three years ago."

He *had* been here a while. She barely recalled the incident. "Did you see it?"

He shook his head. "Heard it. I was resting. Don't sleep too well. So I tend to nap during the day." He chuckled, a pleasant—although slightly rusty-sounding—tone. "Not like I have to be somewhere else."

She sidled a couple of steps downwind of him. If she was to believe him, she had to know if he was under the influence of alcohol. She sniffed the air.

His mouth tipped up. "Don't drink. Although the devil spirit is what brought me so low."

"Devil spirit?"

"Alcohol. Cheap wine, to be exact. Ironic, isn't it, that something used in the Lord's sacraments should be such a snare. Not that I started with that."

"No?"

"No. I drank because I liked the taste. Then I drank more because I liked the peace I felt. Then I drank even more because my wife left me because I was drunk all the time. Had all the peace I wanted then."

"Right."

She'd made a mistake coming down here by herself. If she could just get back to her car—

He glanced up the hill then back at her. "Know what you're thinking. Another drunk. Get out of here." He shook his head. "Haven't touched a drop in almost four years."

"Why do you stay here?"

"Only place I can call my own."

"Can you tell me what you saw? Or heard?"

He peered at her. "You with the cops?"

"No. My husband was hurt in the accident."

"Sorry to hear that." He indicated a couple of logs circling the fire pit. "Have a seat, and I'll tell you what I saw."

She hesitated, but Bradley stepped forward, pulling her with him. She had no choice but to join him.

When they were settled, the drifter nodded. "Name is Denver."

Bradley pointed a thumb at his chest. "I'm Bradley. And this is my grandma Carly."

Denver nodded. "Young to be a gramma."

"I married a grandfather."

He smiled. "You've done that one a time or two. Good response."

She settled on the log, revising her former opinion of the man. She was going to like him. "Where you from, Denver?"

He squinted up at the sky. "Here, there, and everywhere, I reckon."

Bradley leaned forward, elbows on his knees. "You're not from Denver?"

"Maybe I am, maybe I'm not. Doesn't really matter where you're from. What matters is where you are, and where you're going." He leaned closer. "Where you going, young man?"

"Home with my grandma. And then home to New York with my parents."

Denver slapped his knee. "Well, doesn't that beat all." He squinted at the boy. "I mean, where you really going?" He straightened and pointed to himself. "Me, I'm going to heaven to be with Jesus someday. When my work is done."

"Mister Denver, how will you know when your work is done?"

The older man sat back. "When I wake up and see Jesus."

Great. Just what she needed. A Bible-thumpin' derelict.

She tried again to get him back on track so she could get her information and leave. "You said you heard the accident?"

"You are a lady with a one-track mind." He chuckled, his beard bobbing on his chest. "Right. Heard a couple of loud clunks, then the car scraped against the guardrail. Then another car pulled up right behind it. Man got out. Went up to the first car. Heard a couple of thumps. Smelled some booze. Cheap stuff, if I had to guess. A few minutes later, sirens."

"And after that?"

"I tucked myself into a ball there in the woods. Out of sight. Didn't want any trouble."

"What did the thumps sound like?"

He shrugged. "I don't know. Thumps. Like giving a watermelon a couple of good raps."

"And the clunks you heard before the accident?"

"Like someone whacking a tree stump with a shovel. Something like that."

"And you're sure about the smell of alcohol?"

He chuckled. "Lady, time was, I could tell you the year and vintage of a wine. Not so much with booze. Never drank enough to know the differences. But the conigers of the stuff sloshed around up there were cheap. Harsh. Almost a chemical smell."

Strange. Why would somebody splash liquor around Mike's car? And what were the thumps that sounded like rapping a melon? Perhaps her husband's head being pounded into the steering wheel? But why? And the clunks beforehand?

If Denver was correct, and somebody was setting her husband up, perhaps that same somebody tried to run him off the road. And when that didn't happen, they tried to kill him and make it look like a drunk driving accident.

Which meant Mike's life was in danger.

"Can you describe this man?"

"Dark hair, white guy. Middle aged. Slender."

Which described about half the population of Bear Cove.

Including Bob Whalen.

"Would you recognize him if you saw him again?"

"I think so. Could pick him out of a lineup, if that's what you're asking."

That was exactly what she was asking.

Which meant that Denver's life could also be in danger. Once the news got wind of the accident and a potential witness, both these men's lives were up for grabs.

She stood and took Bradley's hand. "Would you like the chance to get off the streets and into some proper housing? Get your life back on track?"

He glanced at the tent then back at her. "I don't think so. I got it really nice here now, what with all the patches, and the sleeping bag." He waited for her reaction then laughed. "Just kidding. Course I'd like that. What you offering?"

"Sounds to me like the pastor in town and you would get along just fine. I bet he could get you a place to live until you earn enough to get your own place. We have a new community center with rooms like a motel for just that."

Denver stood and bowed. "After you."

$$$

An hour later, and Denver was ensconced in a room at the community center, which was housed at the rear of the town building. He and the pastor hit it off right away, and the pastor already had work lined up for him. Seemed Denver had a knack with wood, and although not eager to answer too many questions about his past—and not for lack of trying on Carly's part—admitted to being a master craftsman. Until the story broke on the news, Denver was safe enough.

A quick call to Tom, and he and Sarah agreed to meet her at the hospital and take Bradley under their wing while she visited with Mike. When they pulled into the parking lot, the boy spotted his parents' rental car. He wriggled in his seat until she stopped and let him out. He ran into their arms, and she left him and went into the hospital.

Mike's room was at the rear of the building, a private affair with a window opening on another parking lot. Neither scenic nor restful, the view seemed designed to encourage patients to get well quickly, freeing up the room for the next ill person.

Which would be fine with her.

She stopped to ask a few questions of a nurse at the station, glad to hear that the surgery went well and his condition remained unchanged. The doctor wanted to keep him in overnight, but would likely release him tomorrow.

All of which was good news to her.

Next Carly paused in the doorway of the room. Hospitals were not her favorite place to visit. The smells, the sounds, the hush-hush, the squeaky soles on highly-polished floors—all of it gave her the willies. She needed to get her mind off the purpose of hospitals—the treatment of sick and dying people— and on to happy images of fresh air and long life.

But neither the nurse's reassurances or her own hopeful thoughts prepared her for her first view of Mike. Skin as pale as the sheets and blanket covering him. His head wrapped in white bandage. Purple and blue bruises on his forehead, cheeks, and chin. An IV with tubes burrowed into the back of his hand, and a machine beeped and chuffed on a stand beside him.

She hurried to his bedside and sank onto the edge of the rubber-coated mattress. His hand lay limp on the blanket, cold to the touch when she wrapped her hands around it.

But his fingers twitched at her touch, and he opened his eyes. Those beautiful deep brown orbs that reminded her so much of dark chocolate.

And his lips curled up in a smile. "Hey, there."

She squeezed his hand. "Hey there yourself."

"Is this what a guy has to do to get his best girl to hold his hand?"

Tears pricked. "I'll hold your hand from now to kingdom come if you'll get up and out of this place."

He shifted his feet then winced. "Might need a rain check on that one."

Her nose stuffed up, and a lump the size of Wisconsin settled in the back of her throat. She swallowed hard and plastered on a smile. "The nurse said you're doing great."

"If this is what great feels like, I don't ever want to feel poorly." He explored his forehead and head with his free hand. "Looks like I did a job on my noggin."

"Something to do with a steering wheel."

"Had my seatbelt on. Just goes to show you. Probably wouldn't have a scratch if I didn't fasten it at all." He closed his eyes and for a minute, she thought he'd fallen asleep. Then he opened them. "Don't remember anything after leaving the house. Except the seatbelt." He scowled. "Where was I going?"

"The home improvement store."

"What for?"

"Locks. You said something to Tom about keeping everybody safe."

He shook his head then groaned. "Note to self. Don't shake head." His mouth turned down. "Don't remember the drive. Did I make it to the store?"

"No. You had the accident on the way out of town. Closed down the road. Which could be a good thing." He groaned, and she patted his hand. "Do you need some pain killers?"

"Not unless I can get you to take them."

"Me? I'm not in pain."

"No, but they'll knock you out. Close the road. That's so you can look into this murder, right?"

"Well, it does help if all the suspects are trapped in town."

"Surely you don't think any of the tourists offed the journalist? Or another reporter did him in?"

She shook her head. "Not really. I have a couple of ideas, and they live here. But I still don't know why he was killed."

Mike looked around the room. "How is Bradley?"

"Great. With Tom and Sarah. Doctor said they want to keep you in overnight but will release you tomorrow morning if all your vitals stay stable."

He pulled her toward him, and she scooted over. "Come here. You're my best medicine."

She giggled. "We don't want your blood pressure going through the roof."

"So what? They can give me something to lower that, but they can't do anything about my need to hold you. Only you can fix that."

She snuggled beside him, content in his arms, grateful his sense of humor returned along with his consciousness.

Soon life would be back to normal, but for right now, she wanted to rest here, safe, thankfulness flooding her every cell.

$$$

Although reluctant to leave Mike, Carly agreed with the nurse who said he needed his rest if he was to go home the next day.

And she needed time to make a phone call or two, not to mention work on her recent assignment.

When she arrived home, the place was empty except for Doc, whose mewling reminded her he hadn't been fed in the last ten minutes. She spooned food into his dish, then made herself coffee while he polished off every last morsel, his tail swishing the floor like the pendulum on a clock. A voice message from the kids said they'd check in at the hospital again on their way home, and would be back in time for dinner. Which they would provide. Nice. They needed some Bradley time, too.

Carrying her mug into her shared office, she sat at her desk and surveyed the papers strewn across the surface. After spending a few minutes reorganizing, she put that project on hold while she made her call.

To the newspaper. Harvey Paulson told Bradley he had a scoop. Something bigger than the eclipse, he said. But first he had to talk to somebody.

His source? Was he going to reveal their identity? Or a person of interest? Somebody sought by the law, perhaps? Or maybe the object of the scoop. To warn them? To get more information? Their side of the story, perhaps?

To blackmail them into keeping quiet? For a price?

Any or all of the answers to these questions could get a person killed, if the stakes were high enough.

And since Paulson was dead, apparently they were.

Which meant that a desperate criminal wandered the streets of Bear Cove.

Did Paulson's murder have anything to do with Bradley's kidnapping? Although not impossible, it would be a huge coincidence for the two not to be related.

Which means her grandson could identify a killer.

But which newspaper to contact? She couldn't recall what his business card said. The closest regional paper was the Portland Press Herald. She'd try there first, and then maybe Augusta. Unlikely he was from anywhere further afield, although he could work for any number of small-town periodicals up and down the coast.

While she waited for the newspaper office to answer, she went through her list of suspects again. The mayor, even though he hired her to look for the missing money. But that was a great way to point her attention in other directions. He had the means to take the money. But motive? Was Paulson blackmailing him?

Evie Mack, the secretary, who might not be telling the whole truth about not having a relationship with the mayor. And what better cover story than to invent a fiancée from out of town that nobody knew. Motive, perhaps, to cover up an affair with the mayor, if there was one.

Paula Akerman, the mayor's wife, could have been approached by Paulson about her husband's affair with Anita and or Evie. Motive, for sure.

Anita, a tiny baby in hand, maybe insisted the father marry her. Whoever the father was. Maybe not the mayor, but who? Bob Whalen? Motive.

Which brought her to Bob. Was it a coincidence that he was the first on the scene of Mike's accident? And what of Denver's belief that the alcohol was added after the fact? But why would he take the money? And why try to frame Mike?

Then there was Gail Sullivan, the most likely suspect. As town treasurer, she had unfettered access to bank accounts, accounting systems, and check books. Opportunity, for sure, but Carly hadn't yet discovered any motive.

"Portland Press Herald. How may I redirect your call?"

The woman's nasally voice bespoke hours of boredom.

"I'd like to speak to someone about one of your reporters, please."

"Which one?"

"Harvey Paulson."

"He isn't employed by us."

"Thanks, I'll try the Kennebec Journal."

"I didn't say he didn't work for us. Only that he isn't an employee. He is what we call a stringer. He comes up with a story, pitches it, and an editor decides whether to pay for him to write it." The voice lowered a notch. "He's dead, you know."

This might be the perfect time to play dumb. "Really?"

"Yes. Murdered in cold blood in a tiny town nobody ever heard of."

Carly gritted her teeth. At least four hundred people—the residents of this tiny town—heard of it. Along with the hundreds who called it home for the eclipse. But now was not the time to give the woman a lesson in either geography or etiquette. "Why would somebody want to kill him?"

"Cops don't know. Might never find out. You know how rinky-dink small-town cop shops can be. All about eating donuts and drinking coffee."

This woman also needed a lesson in small-town police

departments. She might not agree with everything Chief Donovan said or did, but not once had she seen him gulping java or quaffing pastries. "Any idea what he was working on?"

"Well, I'll give the Berry Town police this much, they already called and asked that question. And I'll tell you the same thing I told him: he wasn't on an assigned project at present. He might have been working on something, but he didn't get to the point of contacting an editor and getting the okay to go ahead." She chuckled. "And if old Harv was one thing, he was a stickler for the approval. Expenses only get paid from the date of said approval, you see."

Carly did see. She thanked the woman for the information and hung up.

Rather than pointing her in the right direction, the conversation only prompted more questions.

And brought her no closer to answering any of the twenty or more she already had.

Chapter 9

The next three hours sped past while Carly compiled a list of entries that would form the basis of her evidence—once she identified the culprit. By the time she finished, her stomach reminded her she skipped lunch, and the knot between her shoulders suggested she'd done enough for one day.

She finished the final note and closed the file just as the phone rang. A glance at the clock confirmed both her stomach and her muscles kept accurate time—almost five o'clock. "Hello?"

"Carly, Chief Donovan here."

"Chief, I've been meaning to call you." And she had. To tell him her family needed protection. "But you go first."

"Wanted to let you know we sent off Mike's blood sample for analysis. Don't have the results back yet. I'll let you know as soon as I do. But I've got to tell you, it doesn't look good."

"Chief, Mike never drinks and drives. I told you that already."

"He smelled like a brewery when they brought him in. I caught the odor from more than twenty feet away."

"I think somebody is trying to frame him."

"I know you want to think that, but who? And why?"

She sighed. "I don't know. Yet. But I'll find out, and when I do, you'll be the second to know."

"I heard all about you and your poking your nose into police business. I won't tolerate you getting in the way. Do you understand?"

Heat rose to her cheeks, and she was glad they weren't in the same room. She might find her fingers wrapped around his neck, shaking him like a rag doll until some sense finally made its way into that thick skull of his.

But thoughts like that weren't lowering her anger threshold or her blood pressure.

She drew a couple of calming breaths. "And if you talked to whoever warned you off me, you'd find out I helped the police solve several crimes in the past. Here, and in other places."

Now it was his turn to sigh. A drawn-out, long-suffering kind of sigh. Like the ones Mike had perfected over his years of marriage to her.

But she wasn't married to the chief. He barely knew her. He had no right to cop an attitude with her.

She giggled at her play on words. Cop an attitude. She tucked it back in her memory. That's one she'd use for sure some day.

"Carly, I don't know how you do it. I've heard some of these stories. You go on a vacation, you get involved in a murder. You visit a friend, you find a body. You plan a wedding, and you're in the middle of a bank robbery. You're a regular soap opera, aren't you?"

"First of all, I've never been involved in a murder. And it's not my fault if I go for a walk and stumble across a body. And if you listened—or read the police reports—I am the only person who believed there was a bank robbery. Everybody else was busy hushing it up."

He chuckled. "Point taken. But that doesn't change the fact that I don't want you getting involved in this murder. Or rather, in its solution. We have it all well in hand."

"Chief, I talked to—"

"Half the town by now. I know. And half of them have called to complain that you're harassing them. Accusing them of murder. Or embezzling. Or simply being in the same town a murder happened in."

"I haven't accused anybody of anything."

"Keep out of it. We are the professionals. If I need help—which I don't—I'll call in the state patrol. Who are also professionals. We don't need amateurs sticking their noses in, disturbing key witnesses and evidence, mucking up our crime scenes."

She harrumphed. "Fine. But don't come crying to me when you can't figure out what's going on." She drew a breath. "Chief, people talk to me. They tell me things."

"No. You ask questions. You pester people. You won't leave them alone until they tell you what you want to know. You cannot take half-truths and innuendoes and intuition and solve a murder. It doesn't work that way."

"Chief, you don't know—"

"Carly, I didn't want it to come down to this, but you're the one who doesn't know. I don't think you know what's going on with your own husband, let alone a complete stranger you met once for less than five minutes. That is, if you're telling me the truth."

The hair on the back of her neck bristled. Was it possible to reach through the phone line and strangle him from here? He'd better hope not. "I don't lie."

"Maybe not, but you don't always tell the whole truth, do you?"

"If I don't, it's because you don't want to hear it. And what did you mean I don't know what's going on with Mike?"

"I suggest you turn your attention from this murder and put it where it's needed. Your husband's health and well-being. He's going to need you."

Her heart raced. Did he know something she didn't? "What are you talking about?"

"Just that a note was found in his pocket with a doctor's name and phone number. In Portland. You might want to find out what that's about. Be there for your husband. Comfort your family. Be grateful for your grandson's safe return."

"And speaking of that, what are you doing to find out who took him?"

"We're working on that, too. In between the murder, traffic control for the eclipse and the mess your husband caused by his drunken spree, we've had our hands full."

"Kidnapping is still a crime, though, isn't it? Even if the victim escapes or is released unharmed?"

"Point taken. And yes it is." Papers rustled. "One other thing. The mechanic who examined your husband's car said there was no mechanical reason for the car to go off the road. Brakes were good. A well-maintained vehicle, he said."

"Yeah, that's Mike. Even takes the car in if somebody dings him in a parking lot."

"Well, that's interesting. Because there is a note about blue paint chips on the rear bumper. But that could have been there prior to the accident."

"Unlikely. He walks around the car every time before he gets in it. If he noticed that, he'd make an appointment to get it fixed."

"Well, that's about all from the report. Thought you'd be interested. What did you want to tell me?"

She almost forgot what it was. And even when she remembered, she didn't know if she wanted to share. Still, this wasn't all about her. "I talked to the homeless guy who lives down the hill from where Mike had his accident. He said—"

"Wait a second. A homeless guy who lives down what hill?"

"From where Mike had his accident. Where all the police tape is blowing in the wind."

A long silence.

Seemed she'd caught him in some shoddy police work, perhaps. "You didn't know there was a man living out there?"

"It's not like he invited us to his housewarming." A deep sigh. "What about him?"

"He heard the accident. Saw a man at the car."

"Right. Mike hit the guardrail. Bob came up after that."

"Denver says—"

"Denver?"

"That's his name."

"Did you ask for ID?"

Now it was her turn to sigh. "Of course not."

"Of course not." The chief's high-pitched mimicking of her voice was not called for. "And you believe a homeless guy named Denver who lives in the woods?"

"He seems like a nice man. And he hasn't always lived in the woods."

"Gotta go."

"Well, since you're so busy with these other things, maybe I could look into—"

"No. Absolutely not. Stay out of it. I'll keep you updated on what we learn. But with regards to the blood test, I don't think you're going to be happy. And I've heard that when you're not pleased, it's like that old saying. If Momma ain't happy, nobody happy." He cleared his throat. "And don't let this old homeless guy fool you. Leave it to us. Please."

The soft click and dial tone indicated he ended the call. Just like that.

Well, if he really thought she'd roll over and play dead—just like that—he had another thing coming.

$$$

After confirming with Sarah they'd be home around six with fish and chips in hand, Carly ventured out again, this time on foot. As she headed for Main Street, she pondered where she might find the cluster of journalists trapped in town by the highway's closure. The diner? The library?

But they weren't in either place.

Instead, when she decided to pop in for a quick visit with Mike, a throng of reporters, digital recorders in hand, accosted her.

One man, his red hair sticking out at all angles, his clothes wrinkled, stepped forward. "Mrs. Turnquist, Tom Sawyer of The Bostonian. How did you feel when the police informed you of your husband's accident?"

She slowed and faced him. "How do you think I felt? How would you feel if the police called and told you your wife was injured?"

"Is that a threat?" He glanced around. "Did you hear that? She threatened to hurt my wife."

More recorders were thrust into her face, and she stepped back. "I didn't threaten his wife. Or him. I answered his question." She raised her hands to block the hands reaching for her. "Out of my way, please. Move back. Give me room."

They parted like a school of minnows before a piranha, then followed her down the hallway toward Mike's room. She paused and shook a finger at them. "Don't come in."

"He's not contagious."

The red haired man again. Apparently the aggressive one.

She peered at him. "No, he's not. But he needs his rest."

"Heard he was drunk. Good thing he didn't hurt anybody else. Drunks should be tossed in jail for life."

"He wasn't drunk."

"Police chief said he was."

"I'm telling you the chief is wrong."

"In everything? Or just in this?"

"In this for sure. Everything? I don't know about that."

The man turned to his peers. "Hear that, guys? She said the chief is often wrong."

"I didn't say that." She stared at each of the dozen or more reporters clustered around her, pinning her against the closed door to her husband's hospital room. If there was a more ludicrous place to be interviewed, she didn't know of it. "If I agree to answer some questions, will you answer some of mine first?"

Red-hair stepped back and looked around. The others nodded or shrugged. He faced her. "Fine. Ask away."

"First, turn off the recorders. This is all strictly off the record."

A couple grumbled, but most complied without complaint.

"Okay. Anybody here know Harvey Paulson?"

A few nods.

"Anybody talk to him before he died?"

An older man, his hair thinning and his waist thickening, stepped forward. "Harv and me go way back. We started out as cub reporters together, fresh out of a journalism program."

"Sorry for your loss."

He lifted one shoulder and let it drop, but his eyes belied his outward appearance of nonchalance. "He went out doing what he loved, you know?"

She offered him a tiny smile. "Right. It's better to wear out than to rust out."

The man considered her words then nodded. "He was excited when I saw him the day before he died. Said he stumbled on a big story."

"A scoop?"

His face brightened. "Yeah, a scoop. Something big that would put this town on the map, he said."

This town was already on the—she gritted her teeth then relaxed her jaw. If she didn't soon figure out who killed Paulson, she'd need a visit to her dentist. "Did he say what?"

A quick shake of the head. "Said he needed to get all his ducks in a row. Got a kick out of that, it seemed. He laughed, said it again. Thought it was real funny."

An overused cliché got a man of words excited? Unlikely. So Paulson's words must refer to the story, or somebody in the story.

"Nothing else?"

"Nope. Now, your turn."

And so, for the next ten minutes, she answered their questions. As patiently as she could. Which wasn't very, because, frankly, they all asked the same questions over and over again. What brand of booze did Mike drink? How long had he been an alcoholic? Had he ever been stopped by the cops before? How many times did he get off with a slap on the hand? After all, everybody knows how small towns work, right?

Statements she denied the veracity of. Insinuations she ignored. Allegations she defended.

When she had enough, she raised a hand. "That's it, folks. Thanks for your patience. Make sure you don't take my words out of context. Don't mention our little bargain, and please, get the name of the town correct."

Although lynching went out of vogue right around the time the town was settled, if residents read about their home in the light these guys seemed to want to paint it, more than one reporter might be bobbing in the harbor in the coming days.

And she didn't need one more thing for the chief to blame her for.

Chapter 10

Once assured that Mike was resting comfortably, she headed home, dodging the more persistent reporters hanging around the lobby. As she walked, however, she thought about the desperation of the killer. And who was safe.

And who wasn't.

Most likely, so long as Bradley stayed near his parents or other adults, the killer wouldn't try to silence him.

But what about Denver?

The man was reclusive by nature, and now that the police knew there was at least an ear witness to the accident, maybe the killer wouldn't try anything.

Then again, maybe he or she would.

Even if the chief didn't think Denver was telling the truth.

She changed direction and headed for the pastor's house. Perhaps he knew where Denver was. The community center temporary housing was under Pastor Jim's supervision, and he kept a close watch on his 'other sheep' as he called those needing temporary housing for various reasons. Even a town as small as Bear Cove had its share of marital disputes, runaways, and transients.

The pastor answered the door and gestured her in. "Denver and I were just enjoying a cup of coffee."

She stepped into the pastor's office and nodded to the homeless man, now clothed in clean clothes, his longish hair combed and his beard trimmed. "Hi, Denver."

"Miss Carly." He stood and shook her hand. "Pastor Jim and I were having an interesting conversation about evidence for the resurrection."

Carly swallowed hard. What had she walked into?

Pastor Jim chuckled. "Turns out Denver here is quite a student of the Bible."

Great. "Is that so?"

Denver nodded. "Yes'm. Went to seminary for half a semester. Lost my job and couldn't stay."

Carly sat. Just what she needed. Surrounded by Bible thumpers.

The pastor quirked his chin toward a coffeemaker on a cart. "Coffee?"

"Sure." Something—anything—to talk about besides God. Although, why she was so averse to the topic, she wasn't certain. Lack of knowledge? Lack of faith? "Just cream."

He poured and doctored her java and handed her the cup. "Denver settled in real nice at the community center."

The homeless man's face relaxed. "I'd forgotten how nice it is to have a real roof over my head. To sleep on a real bed. Not always be cold."

She sipped her coffee. Hot and creamy. Just the way she liked it. "How long have you lived rough?"

He shrugged. "Not sure. Seems like forever."

The pastor leaned forward. "But you are educated. And you discovered a real talent for working with wood."

Denver smiled. "Didn't know about that until I picked up that piece of board and knew what to do."

Carly set her cup down. "I want to hear that story."

Pastor Jim nodded toward the older man. "It's his tale to tell."

Denver crossed one leg over the other His mismatched socks might have looked ludicrous on another, but on him, they were perfect. One brown, one white. Maybe he'd start a new trend. "There was a broken window at the community center. Kids, I guess. Anyway, I looked around, found a hammer and a piece of plywood, a few nails, and in no time, had that window covered." He uncrossed his legs and recrossed them in the opposite direction. "While I was a-pounding those nails in, it's like a window into my memory opened. I saw myself making a cabinet. So I asked for more wood, and I made one for my room, to put my stuff in."

Pastor Jim nodded. "When I saw what he was doing, I asked if he needed anything else. Pretty soon he was making drawers, installing hooks, and doing some fancy woodwork—"

"Routering."

Jim nodded at Denver. "Right. Routering. On the doors. Made them look like they were store-bought. A coat of stain, and we have a masterpiece."

Denver's mouth lifted in a half-smile. "Like to pay my way. So for every night I stay, I'll make another cabinet for one of the other rooms."

Carly picked up her cup again. "At that rate, I might want you to come live with us and build us some cabinets."

He nodded. "Have hammer and nails and router, will travel."

Now that he seemed relaxed, this might be the time to find out more about him. "Do you think that's what you used to do? Build cabinets?"

He shook his head. "Don't know. It's all like looking through a fog. Sometimes I see a little bit, then the fog rolls in and I can't see nothing. All I know is what I know."

"No idea where you used to live? Or why you left?"

He uncrossed his legs and planted both feet on the floor, his shoulders tense. "No. Like I said, don't remember nothing."

Carly glanced at Pastor Jim, who responded with an almost imperceptible shake of his head. Was he saying *don't push*? Or *don't believe him*? Either way, she wasn't giving up yet. "But you do remember the day of the accident?"

He blinked a couple of times. "Accident? Which one? There's always accidents out on that highway." He stood. "Need to go for a walk. See you later."

What the—Carly couldn't believe he'd be so cavalier about what he saw—or rather heard. He seemed so anxious to help earlier.

So what changed?

After the door closed behind him, she turned to the pastor. "Any idea what that was all about?"

He shook his head. "He's been pretty quiet about his past so far. Which isn't unusual for these types. Often they're running from something. The law, maybe. A warrant, perhaps. An unhappy marriage. Broken family. Sometimes there's no reason at all. Something just snapped one day and they walked away from everything."

"Can we get him to talk to us about it?"

"Maybe. Maybe not. But it will be on his terms. We can't push, or he'll do what he always does. He'll leave. It's what they do."

"I need him to stick around. He heard the accident. Saw a man come up to Mike's car and splash alcohol around. Somebody is trying to frame Mike, and I want Denver to identify him."

"Well, he said he spent a few hours today walking around town. Maybe he saw the guy then."

Her heart clanged like a noonday bell. "If he did, he could be in trouble."

"Or maybe he's hoping to sell his information to the highest bidder. You didn't offer him money or anything, did you?"

The very thought was ludicrous. Her entire professional reputation and credibility for court testimony would be out the window if word got out she paid a homeless man to give evidence to get her husband out of a jam. "No. I wouldn't do that. Couldn't."

Pastor Jim nodded. "Didn't think you would." He leaned forward, elbows on his knees. "Carly, you and I don't know each other very well. So I hope you don't think I'm stepping over a line here."

"I'll let you know if you tread on my dance shoes."

He smiled, crinkles appearing at the corners of his eyes, like he spent a lot of time outdoors. Or smiling. "I saw the deer-in-the-headlights look when I mentioned Denver's knowledge of the Bible and our discussion of the resurrection."

Maybe he was edging close to her toes. She squirmed in her chair. "I'm not sure where I stand with all that, Pastor. I know it's your job to talk about God and all that religious stuff, but I'm not ready right now."

He jutted out his bottom lip and nodded. "Understood. When you are ready, you know where to come."

"I do. My daughter and her family are religious."

He sat back and chuckled. "Funny. You said 'religious' twice now. I think you'll find that I'm not the least bit religious, as you call it."

"Well, then, spiritual."

"Oh, we're all spiritual, because that's how God created us. It's what makes us different than the animals. And our spirit longs to connect with God. But religion gets in the way."

"I thought it was all about religion."

He folded his hands in his lap. "Nope. It's all about relationship."

"I'll think on that, Pastor Jim."

"You do that."

And she would.

Just not today.

$$$

Bradley spun around on the stool at the counter while his parents waited for their order. Fish and chips. One of his favorite meals. And especially with gravy and stuffing and green peas.

He stopped the spin and waited for his vision to clear before tugging on his father's sleeve. "Dad, can I have some chicken wings, too?"

His father smiled down at him. He liked when his dad smiled. All the little crinkles at the corner of his eyes wadded up together, lifting his father's cheeks and his mouth at the same time. "I don't think you'll have room, but sure. We can always have leftovers, right?"

Bradley responded to a high-five, and turned around to survey the other customers. Most sat in booths or at tables, chowing down on the really good food. Miss Victoria, the waitress, carried a tray of food to one table in the corner. When he grew up, he'd like to work in a place like this.

All the free fish and chips he could eat.

The door opened, blowing in the man he and Gramma Carly met earlier today. The man who lived in the tent up off the highway. Ooh, he wouldn't want to live in a tent. No siree. He much preferred a warm bed, clean clothes, and hot food.

Living in a tent was too much like how he and his first dad used to live, except they usually lived in a car. But he liked how he lived now.

The man sat at the end of the counter, his elbows on the top, his feet hooked on the little bar thing that Bradley couldn't quite reach on his own stool. He glanced up at his father, who chatted with Miss Victoria and his mother, before sliding off his stool and down to the one beside Mr. Denver.

That was a funny name for a man. Like the city. They studied the state capitals in geography, so he knew where Denver, Colorado was.

He nodded to the man. "Hi, Mr. Denver. What'cha doing?"

"Nothing."

"They have good food here."

"Uh-huh."

"We're getting some to take home for dinner. Want to come to our place?" Surely his parents wouldn't mind. Gramma Carly already knew him, and he'd be willing to share his food with the man. "We can share."

A deep rumble like a cough came out from Mr. Denver, and at first, the sound kind of scared Bradley until he realized the older man was laughing. Eyes crinkled, mouth turned up, just like his dad's. "Thanks, but no thanks."

They sat in a comfortable silence for a minute or so while Bradley tried to think of something to say. Something that let Mr. Denver know he wasn't just a little kid. That he knew things, too.

Finally, he had an idea. "I used to live in a car with my first dad."

The older man looked over at him, studied him a moment like he was seeing him for the first time. "You did, huh? How long? A weekend? A week?"

"No, sir. For four years. All the way from when I was just a kid." He puffed his chest up. "I was real helpful. My dad said so. I'd find wood for a fire. And I could get folks to give me money just by saying I was hungry."

Mr. Denver nodded. "Yeah, that's easy to do when you're cute. Not so easy when you get big like me." He glanced over at Bradley's parents. "He doesn't look like the type to live in a car."

"Oh, not my dad. My first dad. He died. And then my mom and dad 'dopted me to be their son 'stead of their nephew."

The homeless man shook his head. "That's getting way too confusing."

"Oh, it's not, really. Although my Uncle Mike is now my Grampa Mike. And my—"

Denver laid a hand on his arm. "It's okay. So tell me more about your life before these fine people found you."

Bradley stuck out his chin like he saw his dad do when his mom said something he didn't like. Worked with her, so maybe it would work with Denver. "They didn't find me. They chose me. There's a difference."

"Ah. I see."

"Can you tell me a story of why you live in a tent?"

Another glance over at Bradley's parents. "Well, I used to have a real tent. One made out of canvas. But it was heavy. And it leaked."

"Doesn't the blanket leak, too?"

"Sure does. When it rains, I get in under the trees and wrap up in the blanket, all snug like. And it's not so heavy as the old tent. But you wouldn't know anything about that. You lived in a car."

"It leaked, too."

"It did? How so?"

"The windows didn't close all the way. Something jammed in them, my dad said."

"How come you were living in a car? Where's your mom?" When Bradley looked over at his mother, Denver clarified his question. "Your first mom?"

Bradley shrugged. "Don't know. She left when I was little. And when my first dad lost his job, he couldn't pay the rent. So we lived in our car. It was only going to be temp—tempry—"

"Temporary."

"Right. Temporary. For a while. But then my dad got into an argument with some guys, and he said we were better off to live in our car so we could move on any time we needed."

A television over the counter caught Denver's attention, and he watched for a moment. The sound was turned down, and the words went so fast across the bottom of the screen that Bradley couldn't keep up with reading. Something about that dead reporter, and the mayor. Who had some kind of trouble. Then Bradley's second-grade picture appeared, along with the word FOUND stamped across it.

Which was really weird, seeing his picture on the television. He glanced around. Nobody else seemed interested in the news, which was good. That wasn't a great picture of him, and he didn't want to remember the man who grabbed him and locked him in the shed. Or the nice lady who let him stay in the house. His Gramma Carly wanted him to remember which house it was, but he kept trying to block it out of his mind. Maybe if he told her which one it was, the man might see him and come and get him again.

No, siree. He didn't want that to happen.

When Mr. Denver stood and headed for the door, Bradley slid off the stool and chased after him, clutching at the tail of his jacket. "Wait, Mr. Denver. You're coming over for dinner, aren't you?"

The man slapped at his hand. "Go away and leave me alone."

Bradley's face heated up as several customers turned and stared. His father stood beside him, hand on his shoulder.

He looked into Mr. Denver's eyes. Where before he saw a friend, now a stranger looked back at him.

As though Mr. Denver didn't even know who he was.

$$$

Walter Akerman paced his living room. Not usually a nervous man, he didn't like the direction things were going.

Not one little bit.

He much preferred being in control of a situation. Which was the main reason he'd gone into politics. Not that he had any grandiose ideas about making changes. No, he simply couldn't abide seeing the way the town—and the state and the country, for that matter—were being run by schmucks with nothing more on their minds than the next photo shoot or press release.

Despite his lack of identifiable civic-mindedness, he was doing good work as mayor. Already businesses were opening on Main Street. The town had retrieved some of its pride in itself. And eventually—maybe not this year or the next—and that invisible barrier that kept the town from growing—small-town mentality— would be replaced by a thriving economy and lower taxes.

That was one of the platforms he stood on to gain the seat, and he would take it on to the state level next year.

Just so long as his past didn't catch up with him.

Who knew that a stupid mistake in college could come back to bite him in the—well, no point in fretting about that now. Everybody had something they wouldn't want their best friend—or their spouse—to know about them. He was no different. At least that error in judgment was an exception, and not a pattern.

He stopped pacing and sat at his desk. Time to make some phone calls. Collect on old favors. Remind folks where the real power in the town—and the state—lay. Money wasn't the only thing that talked.

Pedigree and family lineage stood for something, too.

Chapter 11

7:30 p.m.

Perhaps this was a fool's chase. And Carly was a fool to pursue it. Denver knew more ways to hide than she knew ways to find him.

If he didn't want to talk to her, that was his choice.

She paused and was about to turn around and go home, get warmed up while waiting for dinner, when a door slammed behind her. She whirled around.

Denver.

Heading in the other direction.

She shrank against the storefront, feeling even sillier. Like something out of a B-grade movie.

Or an A-list blockbuster.

He strode along the street, away from her, head down, hands in his pockets, muttering. To himself, she supposed, since there wasn't anybody else around.

Where was he going?

Only way to find out was to follow him.

Within minutes, she had her answer. His destination was the park. The same park where Harvey Paulson was murdered. Was he returning to the scene of his crime? No, that only happened on television, or with weird, psychotic serial killers.

She slowed. She didn't know Denver. Not really. Only what he shared. Which wasn't much. He didn't seem like a killer, but then again, in her experience—limited though it might be—killers often appear benign. Harmless. Good people who love their dog and help little old ladies across the street.

Until the truth comes out.

She shivered. Maybe she should forget this and go home. After all, if Mike knew what she was doing, he'd have a conniption.

Or worse.

Then again, if he wasn't the killer, Denver could be walking into a trap.

Or worse.

She couldn't let that happen. Already one innocent man—Mike—was under scrutiny for something he didn't do. And perhaps Bradley could be in danger because he saw the man who kidnapped him. Not to mention that Denver saw the man who tried to frame Mike.

She crept along in his wake, leaving a good fifty feet or so between them, grateful for the shadows cast by the setting sun against the trees. The path through the park wound amongst some of the larger stands of trees, for which she was grateful. If he turned around, she could melt into the underbrush.

But he didn't. Apparently his conversation with himself was so absorbing he didn't even notice her behind him. Not even when she inadvertently kicked a pebble, sending it skittering along the asphalt surface. That was a heart-stopping moment. She froze, one foot lifted, like a bird dog pointing to the fall. She chuckled. Another lesson from her father.

Ahead, Denver veered off the path. She glanced at her shoes. Great. Her white sneakers. If she knew she'd be tramping through the woods, she'd have worn her old black pair.

Which reminded her of Harvey Paulson. He was wearing brown sneakers. Had he known he'd be off the path? Is that why he didn't wear better shoes? Then again, maybe they were comfortable.

Maybe they were his only pair.

She made a mental note to look into that.

Carly peered between a couple of maple trees, their fall colors already showing in the golden hues. Denver paused on a small bridge over a creek running down to the harbor. He leaned with his back against the railing. Which seemed a strange position.

Unless he didn't trust the person he was meeting.

In less than a minute, footsteps crunched along the path beyond the bridge. She held still, not wanting to disrupt the moment. Her heart raced, and she itched to wipe sweating palms against her jeans, but refrained.

Any movement, no matter how small, could spook the pair.

Denver stepped away from the railing and nodded to the person coming toward him. The newcomer—a man? He certainly seemed tall enough—withdrew something from a pocket. Carly's breath caught in her throat. Would she be forced to jump in and save

Denver? Or should she run for help? She glanced around. Why hadn't she thought to bring her cell phone with her?

She turned her attention back to the pair. Denver accepted a small packet—envelope-sized or so—and shoved it into his jacket pocket, then the two turned in opposite directions and walked away. Carly waited until Denver passed her while she hid under the branches of an old fir tree, then crept across the bridge to follow the other person.

He—she—was gone. She traveled another twenty feet or so along the seldom-used path without seeing or hearing any evidence that anybody passed by in the last year.

But she knew what she saw.

Well, if she couldn't follow that stranger and find out what was going on, she'd track down Denver.

But by the time she returned to the main path, he was nowhere in sight. Which way might he have gone? Deeper into the park? Where the path diverged at least three times before ending at the other entrance. And from there, he could go any number of directions.

If he retraced his steps, he might return to the community center. Or the pastor's house. Or his camp out on the highway. Or somewhere else.

Honestly, the man was like the wind. Nobody knew where he went or where he came from.

Perhaps not even Denver himself.

Well, dinner would be cold if she didn't go home. Tom and Sarah would wonder where she was. And worry. And they might call Mike to see if she was at the hospital with him, and then he'd worry, too.

No, the most sensible thing would be to go home. Pretend this never happened.

She'd check in with the pastor by phone.

Just this one time, she'd be sensible.

Not that she had any intention of making that a habit.

$$$

As expected, Tom and Sarah were worried. A little. At least, that's what they said. But the fish and chips were good. Fish crispy and flaky, chips soggy. Just the way she liked them.

And apart from Bradley seeming a little quiet and withdrawn, everybody else was in good spirits. Mike should come home from the hospital tomorrow, and the kids accepted her story that she felt like a walk, although Tom's eyebrow did raise in that way that reminded her so much of his father. Almost as though he didn't quite believe her.

Well, she got some exercise, so it wasn't exactly a lie. And she was ravenous, which was good, since Bradley's appetite seemed to have disappeared along with his good humor.

But perhaps that was to be expected. After all, the child had just gone through a traumatic experience. Kidnapped. Someone he knew murdered. But it did seem as though something else was on his mind.

After polishing off her own dinner and half of his, she patted his shoulder and headed for the fridge. "Got room for ice cream?"

He exhaled, a long, drawn out breath. "No thanks."

His mother reached across the table and held his hand. "Something you need to talk about, little man?"

He toyed with a fry. "Why do people pretend to be your friend then change?"

His father propped his chin on his hands. "Like who?"

"Mr. Denver."

Sarah sat back. "The homeless guy?" She glanced around the table. "The man we saw at the diner?"

Tom nodded. "You seemed to be getting along pretty well until he left. What happened?"

Carly returned to the table with the container of ice cream, bowls, spoons, and chocolate syrup, then dished up dessert. "He seems like a nice man. But he doesn't like to answer too many questions."

Bradley nodded. "He was nice. We talked about living rough."

Carly handed him a bowl. "Then what?"

"I said he could come to dinner." He glanced at his parents. "That was okay, wasn't it, Mom and Dad? He looked hungry."

Sarah cast her eye on her husband then back to her son. "You should always check with us first."

Tom nodded. "But that would be okay since Gramma Carly knows him."

"But he started to leave, and when I asked him if he was coming, he slapped my hand."

Carly sensed Tom bristling, so she intervened. "Did you touch him?"

"Just his sleeve."

"Some people don't like to be touched."

"He looked at me like he didn't know who I was."

Sarah picked up the explanation. "But we don't know where he came from, or what happened to him in the past. Maybe somebody hurt him, and you might have startled him. Do you understand?"

He nodded. "I guess so." He turned to Carly. "But then he left and I don't know where he went. Will he be all right? I don't want him to be alone-ly."

Carly chuckled at his misuse of the word. "He'll be fine. The pastor found him a nice place to stay." She finished the last of her frozen treat. "Speaking of which, I need to make a call to the pastor."

Tom stood and gathered dishes. "My turn to clean up tonight."

Carly left the kitchen and went to her office, then dialed the pastor's number. "Hi Pastor Jim. Did Denver come back to his room?"

"No, he hasn't, and I'm getting worried."

Without explaining why, she filled him in on seeing him at the park, figuring that was all he needed to know right now. "Maybe I'll take another walk downtown and see if I can find him. My grandson said he chatted with him at the diner after he was at your house, and he seemed fine until he touched the man's arm. Then Denver reacted poorly. Bradley said it was like the man didn't know him."

"I suspect he has some untreated mental health issues. Or perhaps he's dealing with PTSD. If you find him, be careful. He could be dangerous."

Carly hung up and returned to the kitchen. "I'm going for a walk." She snagged her cell phone from the counter and tucked it into her jeans pocket. "Back in about twenty minutes."

Tom peered at her. "Another walk? What are you up to?"

She jabbed her chest with a thumb. "Moi? Up to something?"

Tom tossed the dish towel on the counter. "The rest can wait. I'm going with you."

"Now, Tom—"

"Don't 'now Tom' me. It doesn't work with Dad, and it won't work on me, either. We go together, or I call Dad and tell him you're up to something."

She sighed. If Mike got involved, she'd be like Rapunzel locked in the tower. And that would never do. "Fine."

He stood, hands on hips. "Fine? Just like that?"

"Just like that. I don't have the time to argue. Get your jacket on. That freshening wind in off the water is chilly."

Within minutes, they rounded the corner onto Main Street. Tom pulled his collar up around his ears. "Glad I listened to you. It is cold."

"You should have remembered. You grew up here."

"That I did. I guess life in the city is making me soft."

She mock-punched his arm. "Not a chance of that."

He clasped the spot and rolled his eyes then groaned.

She laughed. "You're so silly. Just like your dad."

"So what are we looking for? Or should I say, who?"

"Denver."

"Why all this interest in a homeless man?"

"Your dad once said I couldn't let every stray get involved in my life, or I'd have a never-ending supply of murderers or victims. Or something to that effect. Maybe I'm just trying to prove him wrong."

"That I would believe. But I don't think it's your only reason." He touched her forearm, and they halted on the sidewalk. "'Fess up, Carly. What's going on?"

"You saw the news. Somebody is trying to frame your dad. And Denver saw that person."

"So he could be in danger?"

"Right. I hoped by convincing him to come into town, we could keep him safe by virtue of having people around. But now that he's disappeared, I'm worried."

"What else is going on?"

She blinked a couple of times. How to not tell the complete truth while not lying to her son? "Don't know what you mean."

"Where did you go earlier?"

"For a walk."

"I don't buy it, Carly. It's like Dad says, you don't like exercise. You don't like sweating. You think increased heart rate is for teenagers in love."

"I followed Denver to the park after he left the diner."

Tom threw his hands into the air. "I don't believe it."

"Let's keep walking."

Over the next couple of blocks, she filled him in on her earlier excursion. At the next intersection, she jogged over and led the way down an alley. Tom slowed her with a touch on the shoulder, then he took the lead, his brow furrowed and eyes narrowed.

In the deepening gloom behind the pharmacy, almost hidden by a dumpster, a pair of shoes poked out.

Carly pointed then ran to the spot, and Tom joined her.

Denver.

With a brown paper bag in his hand.

She picked it up and sniffed. "Smells like alcohol."

Tom slapped the older man's cheek, gently at first, then more briskly. "Denver, wake up. It's Tom. Wake up."

The homeless man's eyes fluttered open a moment, not focusing, then rolled back into his head. The bottle clattered to the ground.

Tom stood. "Call 9-1-1. This is serious. He might have overdosed."

Not Denver.

Unless she drove him to it.

$$$

The whole thing was like a poorly staged farce. Carly and that nosy son of hers just happening upon the old homeless guy. Pretending like they knew what they were doing. Slapping the man's face. Sniffing the bottle.

That was probably a mistake, leaving the bottle there. Then again, how could a person know somebody would stumble upon the guy before the deed was done? What were the chances? It was like she had some kind of dead body radar or something. Maybe what folks said about her was true—a human cadaver dog.

Except judging the level of activity—the ambulance, the medic, the police chief—the old fella wasn't dead.

Better stay out of sight. Good thing this alley had no lighting. Lots of trash, though. The stench was enough to choke a vulture sitting on an outhouse. Probably meant there were rats, too. Skittering in the corner over there. A cat yowling at the moon. Something else gnawing on a bone over in that corner.

Time to get out of here. The medic loaded the old guy into the ambulance. On his way to hospital, no doubt. Good. That meant they'd both be in the same place. Easy to get a two-for-one that way. The nosy accountant's husband, and now the homeless guy.

Talk about a set-up.

Chapter 12

Tom paced the length of the alley, staying way out of reach of the police chief and the ambulance guys. His dad was right. Carly *was* a full-time job. Yet there was no doubt about it—her hunch was right this time. Denver was in in trouble.

Within minutes of her call to the police, the chief pulled up, with the ambulance close behind. Right now, Carly and the chief stood near the still-prone body of the homeless man while two paramedics knelt beside Denver, checking him out.

Several times she inched closer, but the chief stopped her with a word twice, and a hand on her forearm this last time.

Tom stifled a chuckle. The chief had his hands full enough with her right now. He'd stay out of it.

The one guy named Greg glanced up. "He's pretty much out of it. We need to get him to the hospital right away."

Carly leaned in and whispered something to the chief, who nodded. "Sounds good. I'll ride with you in case he comes to and can tell us what happened."

The other paramedic, Stan, chewed his bottom lip a moment before nodding. "Not usual protocol, but fair enough."

Carly stepped forward. "Chief, can I—"

He shook his head and gestured toward Tom with his chin. "No. You ride with Tom if you want to come to the hospital. But since you're not family, don't be surprised if they won't let you in to see him." She opened her mouth, but he raised a hand, palm facing her. "Regulations. But I'll let you know as soon as we know something."

She sighed but stayed where she was, shoulders slumped.

Tom stepped forward. "Come on. Let's go get the car so we're not wandering the streets at all hours. The cops might pick us up."

She offered him a wan smile. "No worries about that. They're busy with a homeless man they found in an alley."

They walked home in silence, and Tom could almost hear the gears grinding in her head as she tried to figure out some things. Not that he understood what. It was as plain as the nose on his face. The homeless guy drank himself into a stupor.

What else could it be?

$$$

Carly kicked a pebble so it skittered across the sidewalk. There was no way Denver drank that alcohol. He was proud of the fact he'd been sober for almost four years. Sure, alcoholics fell off the wagon every day. Maybe the stress of seeing the accident. Maybe the change in his living conditions.

Maybe she pushed too hard with all her questions.

Or maybe somebody set Denver up like they tried to set Mike up.

She huffed at the thought. If so, that person didn't have much imagination, trying the same trick on two people.

Two seemingly unrelated people.

When they reached the house, they tiptoed in. Sarah lay curled in a ball on the sofa, an afghan pulled over her. Carly snagged the car keys from the hook by the door and then backed out, almost tripping over Tom. She rolled her eyes at him. "You are as bad as your father." She kept her voice low so they didn't disturb Sarah. "Do you want to drive?"

"Always."

Honestly, he *was* just like his dad. An ache developed in the base of her throat at the thought of Mike in the hospital. Well, maybe she could kill two birds with one stone. She'd drop in and see him while they waited for an update on Denver.

If she could get past the nurse. It was well past visiting hours.

Tom navigated the dark streets with skill, and within a few minutes, they pulled into the hospital parking lot. Together they made their way into the emergency area. After checking with the clerk, they sat and waited.

For about two minutes. By that time, her feet itched to carry her to Mike's room, and she stood, decision made.

The chief could hunt her down when he was ready.

"Carly."

Had she conjured up his voice with her thoughts? She turned.

Nope. There he stood. In the flesh.

"Chief."

"Got an update on Denver. Doc says he overdosed on sleeping medication. Likely in the bottle. Bruises on his lips and mouth indicate the bottle was forced in. A nasty lump on the back of his head, too. Whoever did this probably knocked him out then tried to make it look like he drank himself to death."

"Sounds like Mike's situation."

"A little. Yes."

"And Denver saw the man who tried to frame Mike."

"Says he did. Hasn't given us any description, though."

Carly returned to her seat beside Tom, and the chief sat opposite. She leaned forward. "Anything else?"

"Found a hundred dollars in twenties, brand new ones, like you'd get from a bank."

"Or an ATM?"

He nodded. "That's a possibility. We can look into that. Not that the local bank has a cash machine, but maybe up on the highway at the mall."

"What kind of sleeping medication?"

"Doc said a name that has about fourteen syllables. Needless to say, I don't recognize it. But he said it's a common brand. Lots of people use it. Can even be bought in an over-the-counter version."

She sighed. "Probably half the town has a prescription."

"Possibly."

"He was at the pastor's house earlier this evening. I talked with him there."

"Did he say anything more about Mike's accident?"

"No. In fact, when I asked questions, he got agitated and left. Bradley said he talked to him in the diner, and again he became upset. Struck out at the boy. Kind of scared him."

Tom nodded. "Right. Sarah and I were there getting dinner. We saw them talking. He seemed harmless enough. After he left, Bradley said they were sharing stories about living in their cars for a while. But suddenly he changed. Bradley said it was like Denver didn't know who he was all of a sudden."

The chief sat back. "Doc said they'd order a psych eval on him. Maybe he has some mental issues. Maybe he killed Paulson. Maybe there wasn't anybody at the accident scene."

"Well, somebody tried to frame Mike."

"Test results aren't back in on that. And even if you're right, maybe this homeless guy is the one who splashed the booze on Mike."

Carly shook her head. "Why would he do that? He didn't know Mike before that. He had no reason to hurt him."

The chief shrugged. "Who knows why crazy people do what they do?"

Carly crossed her arms over her chest. "I don't think so. He seemed pretty normal when we talked with him in the woods below the highway. And the pastor said they had a great discussion about the Bible before I got there."

Tom peered at her. "So what do you think happened tonight?"

"I think he went to the park to meet the man he saw at the accident. Maybe to blackmail him. Maybe to warn him he was going to tell the police what he saw. He seems to have a high sense of justice, so maybe he hoped he could convince the guy to turn himself in."

The chief shook his head. "That doesn't sound like someone who'd take money. Sounds more like somebody who was being bought off."

Carly had to agree the behavior seemed out of character for the kind of man she hoped Denver was. "Maybe he took the money on the pretense of keeping quiet?"

Tom pursed his lips. "And you think this guy—or gal—then decided to kill him? That's pretty far-fetched. Even for you, Carly."

"I know. It does sound desperate. But we do have a dead journalist."

The chief cleared his throat. "And you think the two are connected?"

"If we assume they are, then we're only looking for one killer."

Chief Donovan shook his head. "But if they aren't connected, and we have two killers, they both might go free because we can't identify one person with a motive to kill two people. Or kill one and try to kill the other."

"Not to mention trying to frame Mike. But why Mike? Was that a crime of opportunity? Or were they trying to get to me? And if so, why? I've had people come after me in the past because of court testimony I was due to give, but I'm not in that situation right now. So why Mike?" She sat back. "It just doesn't make sense."

The lawman pulled out a notebook and jotted down something. "So let's work at this from two angles. How about I keep looking for why someone wants to kill a homeless guy, and you keep asking questions about who would want to kill the journalist? That way, if they're the same person, we'll wind back to the same suspect. And if it's two different people, we'll leave no stone unturned."

Well, this was unexpected. "Are you deputizing me, Chief?"

"Not officially. And if anybody asks, I'll say you are on your own."

She harrumphed. "And if I find the answer, you'll take the credit?"

"That we will share." He pointed at her. "I already know that half the town believes you're the true brains and detective skills behind our police. I don't know how many little old ladies remind me of all the cases you've solved."

It was nice to be appreciated. And acknowledged. But she wouldn't gloat.

At least, not right now.

Right now, she had a killer—or two—to find.

Because despite his carte blanche release for her to find Paulson's killer, that didn't mean she wouldn't keep looking into the attempt on Denver's life.

$$$

Carly stood over her husband as he slept in his hospital bed. He hadn't stirred since she entered his room almost ten minutes before. Laying there, he looked so peaceful.

And vulnerable.

Which made her think of Denver.

She stepped out into the hallway and dialed the chief. "Do you think we should have somebody guard Denver's room? I mean, whoever tried to kill him tonight might try again."

"Nurse Jones is on duty. Nobody gets past her."

Carly agreed. The woman was built like a Sherman tank and had hands the size of hams. Nobody messed with her.

After she disconnected, she returned to her husband's room. Still he slept on. Watching him reminded her of the strange phone call he had with Dr. Nick. Did Mike have a health concern? One he wasn't sharing with her? She'd have to ask Tom if he knew something.

In a roundabout way, of course.

No point in him worrying more about his dad than he already did.

She headed for the waiting area to meet Tom, who lounged in a chair, head back, snoring softly. She nudged him. "Did you want to go in and see your dad?"

Tom rubbed his bleary eyes. "Is he awake?"

"No."

"I'll pass for now then. We both need our sleep." He looked outside. "It's raining. I'll go get the car and pick you up at the door. No point in both of us getting wet."

While she waited, her phone buzzed in her pocket. She checked the CALLER ID. NO NUMBER AVAILABLE. Strange. "Hello?"

A gravelly voice crackled in her ear. "Back off."

"What?"

"You heard me. Back off. Or else."

The line went dead.

Her heart raced and her mouth went dry. Who had her cell number? Dozens of people, probably, but none she could call to mind who would threaten her.

And back off what?

The town audit?

Finding the person responsible for taking Bradley?

For running her husband off the road then framing him?

The journalist's murder?

Or the attempted murder of Denver?

She had so many things going on she felt like a juggler trying to balance knives, flames, champagne flutes, and eggs. One misstep, and she'd have a huge mess and likely get hurt in the bargain.

But perhaps that's exactly what this person wanted.

Chapter 13

10:05 p.m.

Carly collapsed onto her bed, grateful for a quiet respite from the day's worries. Tom and Sarah slept in Denise's old room, while Bradley snoozed in his father's room.

At last, all was quiet.

All except her mind.

She glanced at the paperback on the bedside table. Although the mystery started out well, by the sixth chapter, she'd guessed whodunit, then confirmed her suspicion by reading the last two.

She was right. As usual. Which made reading the rest of the book a moot point, at least in her mind.

And she hadn't taken time out to visit the library for another.

Maybe there was a good movie on the television. She punched the button on the remote and fluffed up her pillow while waiting through a series of commercials.

A newscaster with the profile of Superman and the clothing sense of a model flashed onto the screen. "And now for local news."

She sighed as the man went on about traffic jams in neighboring towns, a water main break in Riverdale, and a petition to lower entrance fees for state parks. Blah, blah, blah.

Her eyes drooped as yet another set of advertisements played.

Just when she figured she'd give up for the night, a familiar name—a very familiar name—caught her attention.

"And from Bear Cove, we have this update. Mike Turnquist, a resident, was in a car accident and alcohol is suspected. Apparently his vehicle went off the road and crashed into a guardrail, narrowly preventing him from going over a cliff. Mr. Turnquist remains in hospital in critical care, while police are investigating the cause. As we said, alcohol is suspected, although a heart attack or some other unidentified health crisis may also have contributed. We'll keep you updated as we learn more. Calls to Mr. Turnquist's home have not been returned."

Carly snatched up the extension sitting beside her and scanned through the list of calls received. One unknown. But that was before the accident, so it couldn't have been the television station.

She gritted her teeth. She didn't know who they called, but it sure wasn't this household. Why would they lie about that? Trying to cover shoddy reporting? Or simply to sensationalize the story?

Well, she'd set them straight. She grabbed the phone book and thumbed through until she located the television station number. But she paused.

One unknown.

Before the accident.

She checked the information again. Right around the time she overheard Mike on the phone with Dr. Nick.

Could he possibly be seeing a heart specialist?

Without a last name or a phone number, she couldn't find out without asking him.

Maybe it was time for some tough questions.

The receiver in her hand rang, and she almost dropped it.

Her heart skipped a beat when she saw the CALLER ID: Bear Cove Community Hospital.

$$$

Mike sighed. Would she never get here? Nurse Jones said she called Carly, let her know he was awake and would like to talk. But had she?

He straightened out the blanket covering him for about the hundredth time in the last ten minutes. His head ached, his shoulder hurt, and there was no way he would try to sit up like that again—way too painful.

He glanced around the room. How long had he lain here? He hated visiting people in hospitals, let alone booking a private room for himself. And why was he here? Right. The accident.

Footsteps hurrying along the hallway alerted him, and Carly entered, lighting the room—and his heart—with her smile.

Although there was a tiny hint of worry at the corners of her eyes.

She perched on the edge of the bed, and he bit back the grunt threatening to escape at the movement. "How are you feeling?"

He lifted one shoulder and let it fall. "About what you'd expect. Achy. Tired."

She planted a kiss on his cheek. "You've slept for hours. Time to be up and at 'em."

He grinned. How he wished that were true. "Doctor says I can go home tomorrow, but that I'm to take it easy."

She snorted. "Like that's going to happen. Unless I have the internet disconnected, you'll be at your desk within five minutes of coming in the front door."

Maybe. "How're things at home?"

"Fine. Tom and Sarah and Bradley have been having fun wandering around town. We haven't found his telescope and camera yet." She edged closer. "Since he lost his stuff while visiting us, I think we should replace it for him."

"Let's wait and see what happens, okay? If anybody can find it, you can."

She peered at him. "Mike Turnquist, are you going soft in the head on me?"

"Huh?"

"You never encourage me to investigate anything."

"Not encouraging you to investigate. Looking for a boy's missing stuff isn't the same as asking questions of a potential murderer."

She nodded. "Speaking of which."

He groaned. "Don't tell me you're involved in another investigation."

"Well, a lot has happened since you took your little vacation without me. The chief actually deputized me."

"And why would he do that?"

Now it was her turn to shrug. "Guess he finally recognized my detecting skills were an invaluable asset to him."

"Or maybe he was just trying to get you off his back."

Her brow drew down. "I didn't pester him."

Mike smiled. "Sure. Now tell me what else you've been up to."

"What makes you think there's anything else?"

"Because you are never a one-bird kind of a detective. You always have multiple pots boiling on the stove."

"That's an awful mix of metaphors."

"But true." He patted the mattress. "Scoot on over here, lean against me—" This time he did grunt when she laid her head against his shoulder. "And tell me what's going on. All of it."

She looked up at him. "So when I went out to the accident scene, I met this homeless guy named Denver. He said he saw a man beside your car after you crashed, and he smelled alcohol. Looked like the guy was splashing it around."

"You said Bob Whalen was there. First on scene."

"Right." She snuggled closer. "Said he was driving past."

"But you don't believe him?"

"Nope. I was at his house less than ten minutes before that. He never said he had to go out. In fact, he made it clear he was going into his darkroom before he th—" She paused then began again. "Before I left."

She was right the first time, no doubt. *Before he threw her out.* "Maybe he remembered something after you left."

"Possible. But there was paint on the bumper of your car. Blue paint. Did you notice it before?"

"No. I don't think so. Although a lot of time is kind of hazy." He quirked his chin toward the wardrobe in the corner. "I think they put my clothes in there. Check my calendar."

She crossed the room and opened the door. His clothes, dusty and smudged with blood and white powder—the airbags deployed—and smelling like a brewery, hung on hooks. In a plastic bag emblazoned with the hospital's name and logo—did they need to advertise?—she found his wallet, belt, keys, shoes, and pocket calendar, which she extracted. "Got it."

She handed it to him, and he flipped to the current month. "Nope, nothing noted here. I didn't see it."

"Maybe it wasn't there when you got in the car."

He tilted his head—just a fraction—in question. "I don't understand."

"A broken taillight and a dent in the rear bumper—a pretty significant dent—means somebody might have rammed you. Denver said he heard a couple of bangs then the crash when you hit the guardrail."

He didn't like where this was going. "Maybe I had a blowout?"

"Nope. Chief said no mechanical reason for the crash."

He sighed. "This is starting to sound like the time you were run off the road."

"Yeah. But that was because somebody didn't want me nosing around town. What have you been up to?"

"Nothing that I know of."

"Unless somebody is trying to distract me from something. Like finding out who kidnapped our grandson. Or who stole the money from the town. Or who killed—no, that can't be right. Paulson wasn't dead yet." She sighed. "And now Denver is in this same hospital."

"Carly, what did I tell you about not getting caught up in every stranger who comes to you with a sad story?"

She sat up. "First of all, he didn't come to me. I found him. And it wasn't his sad story, because he hasn't shared that with me. I was trying to keep him safe because he said he can identify the man he saw outside your car."

"Why is he in hospital?"

"We found him passed out in an alley. The doctor said he overdosed on sleeping medication. And alcohol. But I don't believe it."

"Why?"

"Denver said he hadn't had a drink in four years. And he found Jesus, so he's trying to turn his life around."

"How long has he lived outside?"

"I don't know. But he and Bradley talked about living in their cars. And the pastor really likes him. Gave him a place to live and all."

A noise at the door and they both turned. A man in a white lab coat nodded toward them. "Sorry to bother you so late, but Nurse Jones said you were here." He stepped into the room. "Do you know the homeless guy?"

Carly stood. "Denver?"

"Right. Well, he's causing a bit of a fuss. The police want him kept here as a material witness until he's well enough to give a statement."

"Sounds like him. Glad to hear he's awake."

"We gave him something to quiet him so he doesn't disturb the other patients for tonight, but he said he won't stay unless somebody named Bradley comes to see him."

Carly glanced back at Mike, and he nodded. "Bradley is our grandson."

"Could you bring him by tomorrow?"

"Sure. What time?"

"After ten should be good. He'll be a little groggy in the morning. If he doesn't mention the boy, I'll make sure to have someone call so you don't waste the trip."

"Fair enough."

The doctor left and Carly sat on the end of the bed. "I should go so you can get your rest." She patted his foot. "Now do you believe that Denver knows more than he's saying?"

"He might be simply a lonely man who connected with our grandson." He pursed his lips. "But I don't think you should leave them alone together."

"I suspect Denver would kill the person who tried to hurt Bradley." She stared at him. "You don't think Denver would hurt him?"

"What do you really know about this man? Only what he's told you. I'm surprised you haven't looked up his entire life story by now. Denver says he could identify the man at my car, yet he hasn't. Why not? Maybe he's just milking this situation."

"I don't think so. Mike, you haven't talked to him. I have. And Bradley really likes him. Although—"

Whenever his wife started a sentence then clamped her mouth shut on the rest put his Spidey senses on high alert. "Although what?"

"Bradley did say he acted kind of strange when he asked him a question. Said it was like Denver didn't recognize him."

"The man probably has mental problems. Likely it's why he's living on the streets. Family got tired of cleaning up his messes. Happens all the time."

"Maybe. But I don't think so."

"Please be careful. This isn't just you we're talking about. Bradley is involved too."

"I'm always careful." She kissed him on the mouth. "That's a promise for when you get home. If you're up to it."

He grabbed at her hand but she snatched it out of his reach. He chuckled. "I'll hold you to that promise."

She blew him a kiss in the doorway, then she was gone.

But the specter of a homeless guy and his grandson remained for a long time.

$$$

Anita Blake checked the IV flow for the homeless guy brought in unresponsive this evening. Although why the town wasted taxpayer dollars was beyond her. He'd get out tomorrow and be back on the streets, drunk in an alley, by the end of the day.

She'd seen it a hundred times before. She sighed. Sometimes the waste of life she saw in this business was such a downer. Why not simply end it here and now? It would be simple. An air bubble in an IV line. Ten mils instead of point one of the sleeping medication. And if that didn't work, a syringe-full of insulin. The guy was homeless, for crying out loud. It wasn't like he had a huge bankroll to pay for his care. Probably his family was tired of picking up the pieces after him. Just think how much good the resources could do for a child with leukemia or a mother with breast cancer, instead of being wasted on—she shook her head.

Logic might tell her she was justified, but she couldn't bring herself to do it.

She was already in hot enough water with that other thing hanging over her head. No point drawing double attention to herself. She liked this town. She didn't want to have to move yet. She was doing good work on the town beautification committee, on the after-school reading and literacy program, and at the community center. She was respected, and so she should be. She worked hard to get where she was, and no silly shortcut would derail her plans again. But neither would she permit anybody else to get in the way. Not like the last time.

Friday, October 29

Chapter 14

Carly sighed when the next morning, at breakfast, the phone rang. Seemed lately as though if she wanted someone to call, all she had to do was pour a cup of coffee.

She picked up the receiver and returned to the table. "Hello."

"Carly, it's Chief Donovan."

She pinned the phone to her ear with one shoulder while slathering butter on her toast. "Good morning."

Across the table, Bradley bit into his PB&J sandwich, leaving a ring of peanut butter across his cheeks.

"What can I do for you?"

"Wanted to let you know you were right."

She paused mid-swipe. "Say again?"

"Got the toxicology back. No alcohol in Mike's system."

She covered the mouthpiece with a hand and caught Tom's eye. "Chief says no alcohol."

Her son rolled his eyes then dug into his scrambled eggs. Like her, he believed his father right from the start.

Still, it was always good to have the cops in agreement.

Not to mention the warm fuzzy feeling she always got when

somebody—anybody—said she was right. Didn't happen often, and she wanted to take full advantage of the opportunity.

She tossed a smile at Sarah then turned her attention back to the phone. "So, what does this mean?"

"Gloating doesn't become you."

"Gloating? Me?"

The chief chuckled. "Mike warned me about you."

"Mike has learned to take me seriously. Particularly when I'm right." She sipped her coffee. "Seriously, what does this mean with regards to the investigation?"

"As much as I hate to say it, I will again. Looks like you were right all along. Someone staged the scene to make it look like Mike was driving drunk. I just don't have a suspect or a motive."

"Which makes protecting Denver all the more critical. He said he could identify the man. Maybe you could use one of those sketch artist kits or something to get a picture."

Chief Donovan cleared his throat. "Well, that's a problem."

"No kit?"

"No witness."

Carly's heart dropped to her toes. "What do you mean?"

"Denver left the hospital last night. After you talked to him."

"I thought Nurse Jones was keeping an eye on him."

"Another emergency came in, and she had to deal with it. A kid with a bean in his ear, apparently. When she checked on him thirty minutes later, he was gone."

"But we need him. He saw who was splashing alcohol in the car."

A long pause. "Carly, there's something you might need to face here."

"What?"

"Denver might not be who you think he is."

"Well, that's easy, because I don't know who he is. Sometimes I think he might not know who he is."

"Right. Which makes his testimony suspect. Inconsistent. Untrustworthy."

She gritted her teeth. "I don't need his testimony. I simply need him to identify the man who tried to frame my husband. I'll take care of the rest."

"Carly."

"You sound just like Mike. Who is lying in a hospital bed because somebody tried to run him off the road. And I intend to find that somebody. If you won't help me, fine. I'll do it myself."

She disconnected the call and set the handset on the table.

"Police."

Sarah slied her eyes toward her son. "Bradley, if you're done, let's go watch a movie."

The boy nodded. "Can we watch *Dinosaur Invasion* again?"

She laughed. "I think you know that one by heart, don't you?"

"Pleeeeeeease?"

Together the two left the room, and within a minute or so, the opening theme music—which Carly thought sounded like a cross between *Jaws* and *Psycho*—filtered in.

She refilled her coffee cup and sat. "Still, it's good to hear the official report agrees with what we already knew about your dad."

Tom patted her hand. "Somehow I don't think that's the end of it, though."

She shook her head. "Denver disappeared again. And the chief says he's not a very good witness."

"He does seem a mite unstable. I saw him in the diner with Bradley."

"Still, I think there's more to him than an old homeless guy. I mean, I bet he's got a family somewhere. Maybe they're looking for him."

He sighed. "And maybe they've written him off."

"But that's really said, isn't it?" She picked up the phone and dialed. "Pastor, it's Carly. Denver left the—oh, he's back at the community center?"

"Yes. Came back late last night. Or maybe it was early this morning. Going on about somebody not keeping their promises. About Bradley?"

"I told him I'd bring Bradley to visit. He said he wouldn't stay in the hospital unless Bradley came. I wasn't going to haul the child out of his bed last night, so I said I'd bring Bradley by this morning. He seemed satisfied."

"I figured it was something like that. I think Denver struggles with his memory."

She toyed with the salt shaker. "He alluded to the fact he's not been drinking for four years. Maybe that has something to do with it."

"Maybe. At any rate, he's here. But it might be best if you stayed away. At least for a day or so. I'll talk to him a bit and see if he has any recollections that might help."

She said her good-byes and hung up then turned to Tom. "Well, that's that. Sounds like Denver is off the deep end again."

Tom sat back. "Maybe he's just scared."

A knot the size of Texas formed in her stomach. "That makes two of us."

$$$

And the next two phone calls she made didn't diminish that knot.

The first, to the regional newspaper editor, while it started out well, rapidly declined. The man, undoubtedly accustomed to making cub reporters cower and politicians cringe, wouldn't back down an inch. "I understand your dilemma, Mrs. Turnquist. But really, we didn't falsely report the facts as we knew them at the time. The words we printed were what the police said or published in their own reports."

"But they were wrong."

"Regardless, it's not like we made anything up."

"No, you'd never do something like that, would you? But you might take a half-truth or an innuendo, then couch it in terms to make it sound more fantastic than it actually is."

"Mrs. Turnquist, please don't get excited. You are making what could be construed as slanderous statements."

"And your paper took suspicions and turned them into fact. That's all it was. The police suspected alcohol was involved. And now the toxicology report proves they were wrong."

"Sorry, can't help you. We are only required to print a retraction when we make a mistake. That didn't happen."

"Legally, perhaps. But what about morally?"

He chuckled. "My dear Mrs. Turnquist, we are the Fourth Estate, and as such, are beyond such relative constraints."

She threw out her final gambit. "If I don't see a retraction in the next edition, I may be forced to hire an attorney to sue for damages."

Another chuckle. "We're talking about yesterday's news here. Even if we did as you asked, nobody will connect the two. The public has already moved on to the next new and juicy bit. Nobody wants to chew on a bone with no meat on it. Good day."

She stared at the handset, dial tone pulsing like an angry horde of bees. Which is just about what she felt at the moment. If she could go through the line. . .

But she couldn't.

She sighed. Next she'd try the radio station. At least that was a local operation. One with not only roots but hands and feet in Bear Cove.

Surely they'd understand the importance of restoring Mike's good name.

But they were of little to no help, too.

No redaction. No updated story. It was almost as though the newspaper editor got to them before she did.

Even when she tried the lawyer ploy.

"Sorry, Carly, no can do." Brett Walker sighed then lowered his voice. "I can't help you. But I can tell you this: follow the money."

"What?"

"I think money is behind the decision, and if you follow the money, you'll find out who is trying to paint Mike's name—and yours—as black as night. That's all I can say. And if you use my name, I'll deny I ever said it. Understood?"

Oh, she understood, all right.

This was no accident. This was no series of missteps escalating out of control.

This was out-and-out war.

$$$

Next on her list of things to do included a walk. Fresh air might clear her head. Ease her frustration.

And perhaps answer a few questions.

When she peeked into the living room, Sarah's head lolled on the back of the sofa while Bradley read a book. "Movie over?"

He glanced up. "Yeah. And Mom fell asleep."

"I see that." She picked up her keys from the hook by the door. "Your dad is headed off to work on his computer. Want to come for a walk with me?"

He tossed his book aside. "Sure. Maybe we can find my telescope and camera."

Grandmotherly guilt welled up in her. She'd barely given any thought to her grandson's loss. Not to mention his traumatic experience. Although, to look at him, he seemed completely recovered. She looped her arm over his shoulders. "Sure, we can keep an eye out."

She resisted the urge to hold his hand—barely—as they walked toward downtown. Outside the bakery, she inhaled deeply. No pecan tarts today. Smelled like bread. They'd stop in on the way back for a fresh loaf.

Bradley veered toward the diner, but Carly had other things on her mind than eating—for a change. She must remember to mention that to Mike when next she saw him. That, plus the fact the chief said she was right, would surely brighten his day and give him something to do.

He could keep an eye out his hospital window for flying pigs.

Simply imagining the look on his face when she shared these two tidbits put a lift in her step, and before she knew it, they stood outside the entrance to the park.

Bradley slowed, his feet dragging. "Do we have to go back in there?"

She glanced around. No way was she letting him out of her sight, but he didn't have to know that. "You could wait for me on that bench over there. I won't be long."

He checked out the wrought iron seat near the gate, then tucked his hand into hers, their fingers entwining like vines. "I'd better go with you. Keep you out of trouble."

She chuckled. "You've been talking to Grampa Mike too much."

He looked up at her, his eyes wide. "I have?" He shook his head. "I don't think so. I miss him. Can we go visit him after we're done here?"

"I think that would be a great idea." She squeezed his hand. "Ready?"

He gave a curt nod.

"You're being very brave, you know."

He straightened his shoulders and led the way. "I know."

They followed the pathways deep into the park, past the playground, past the picnic tables, toward the soccer field and the harbor. Carly kept up a steady chatter, asking Bradley if he recalled going this way, if he remembered playing on the swings, or sitting to take a rest at a table. Once she broached the subject of his duffle bag.

"Is it possible you set your bag down then walked away without it?" She laid a hand on his shoulder. "We won't be angry with you if you lost it, you know."

His hand, now sweaty, clasped hers. "I didn't lose my stuff, Gramma. That man took it. The one who grabbed me."

But he still couldn't describe the kidnapper.

She sighed. Funny how the brain worked. Just like Denver, he said he'd recognize the man if he saw him again. He just couldn't take the picture apart, as it were, to describe all the parts.

When she reached the soccer field, she veered down toward the edge of the bank leading to the path where she found Paulson's body. Bradley happily followed her, pointing out a robin or an elm tree. She took this as a good sign that nothing bad happened here.

When they reached the spot, Bradley confirmed her suspicions.

"This is where I saw that man. The one we met at the bus station. He said he was meeting somebody."

"Right. Mr. Paulson."

"He died, didn't he?"

"Yes, he did."

Bradley stared at the spot. "Do you think he and Daddy are having fun in heaven? I think Daddy would like him, don't you?"

She wished she had the words to answer his question the way he needed it answered.

But for once, she was speechless.

She pulled him to her side. "I think your daddy would absolutely like Mr. Paulson. They both liked you, didn't they?"

He nodded then pointed. "Look, there's an eagle."

She followed where his finger indicated to the top of a tree. It wasn't an eagle. It was an osprey. But she didn't have to discourage him by setting him straight.

A flash of color caught her eye, and she froze. Bradley wandered off a few feet to study a small bush covered with bright red berries. What was that? Or who?

A reflection of sunlight off glass.

Binoculars?

No, a camera. Trained on the same osprey at the top of the spruce.

And when the instrument lowered, a face.

Bob Whalen.

She turned to grab Bradley to look at the man, but he was out of reach.

And when she turned back, the paramedic turned amateur photographer was gone.

As was her chance for an unofficial identification.

She huffed.

Would nothing work out for her today?

Chapter 15

After stopping in at the bakery for two loaves of fresh-baked bread—one white, one whole wheat—and making certain Bradley was well-occupied with a book, Carly settled in at her computer and pulled up the Internet. She had a list of suspects, but decided to begin with Anita, mostly because she was certain the woman was hiding something.

Well, if the crime scene wouldn't tell her more, perhaps the Internet would. Not that it knew everything—after all, it was neither a female nor an encyclopedia. But it cut out a lot of steps, didn't mind being asked awkward questions, and didn't keep regular business hours.

But even after paying for a complete report on the nurse—including her criminal report—nothing of interest turned up.

Next was Bob Whalen. And for only another buck ninety-nine she could know all the secrets Bob was trying to hide—which apparently was limited to his website for his photography. She scanned through several screens purporting to be his portfolio, filled with mostly tourist-shop images of seagulls, ospreys, and sparrows, with the occasional robin and woodpecker thrown in for good measure.

Not surprising, since these were common in the area.

No listing of clients, past or present. No reviews or comments.

Seemed more of a hobby site than a true business.

But wait—there was another website.

She clicked on the link and waited for the page to load. Bob Whalen for State Congress.

Interesting. She hadn't heard anything about that around town. And he hadn't mentioned he hoped to give up paramedic-ing and photography and trade it all in for a life in the Maine legislature.

She read through the accolades from people she didn't know or recognize, all purporting to be business and political leaders in the region, even as far away as Augusta. Then she went through the list of contributors, which numbered about a dozen. Again, nobody she knew or knew of.

Then again, this was small-town politics. He made a lot of promises based on experience she couldn't confirm or deny, to bring about changes, such as lowering taxes, increasing social benefits, improving highways, and "bringing a fresh, young face into the hallowed halls of history".

A direct quote from him, apparently.

A lot to ask of a black horse in the political race.

Next she checked into Mayor Akerman, not that she really suspected him. Still, no point in jumping to conclusions. According to Mike, her only form of exercise most of the time.

Another offer of a complete record, which she disregarded. Then—what? Another website? Well, that made sense. He was the mayor of the town, after all. And apparently anybody could get a site with their name on it. She made a mental note to check her own later.

She typed in Walter Akerman For State Congress—what were the odds that—yep, there it was. He was running for the same office as Bob Whalen. But right there, at the top of the page, below his smiling face, a notice: WALTER AKERMAN HAS WITHDRAWN HIS CANDIDACY FOR PERSONAL REASONS.

She harrumphed. Personal reasons? What was that all about? The compromising photo? The allegations of an affair between him and his secretary? The town's missing money? The possibility of being arrested for murder or attempted murder?

Maybe that's where the funds went—to support his campaign.

Of course, the same could be true for Bob Whalen. He had access to the bank account, too.

She went to Akerman's list of contributors page. Nothing. Which seemed strange. How could he even think to run a campaign without funding?

Unless he was stealing it.

Or didn't want anybody to know where the money came from.

Maybe one of his backers was somebody shady.

And what about Bob? Were the names of his contributors genuine? After all, he owned the website. He could publish whatever he wanted. And nobody would be the wiser.

Well, she'd get to the bottom of this.

No matter how far she had to dig.

$$$

After seven rings, Carly hung up. Bob wasn't home. Or he wasn't answering his phone.

She called the mayor next, waiting a few minutes while Evie connected her. Listening to the canned music through three songs made her wonder if he'd ever answer, when his politician's kiss-the-baby-shake-your-hand greeting came on.

"Carly, and how are you this fine day?"

She held the phone an inch or so from her ear. "Fine, Mayor."

"And how is the audit coming?"

"Okay. I have a couple of questions."

"Shoot." His chair squeaked. "Ha, ha. Then again, as often as you find bodies, you might think I'm encouraging you."

Ha, ha, ha. Too funny. Not.

She gritted her teeth. If she didn't figure this case out soon, she'd need to see her dentist. "You were running for State Congress."

A sharp intake of air suggested that wasn't the question he expected. His chair squeaked again. "Yes. Past tense. I decided to withdraw my nomination."

"Because?"

"For personal reasons."

"Such as?"

She suspected he didn't want to answer which was why he was being so evasive. But she intended to know the truth.

"I didn't want my family in the spotlight given the recent untrue allegations."

Another evasion. "But don't you think your withdrawal might confirm the rumors? And validate the lie?"

He sighed. "I don't care. I just didn't want my family dragged through the mud."

"Unless there's some truth to the picture?"

"No. There isn't. But somebody wants me out of the way. So I'm stepping aside."

"But Mayor, if that person is an opponent, aren't you giving in to somebody who would win this campaign by smearing you? What kind of a representative is that? Shouldn't the public know?"

"Carly, perhaps you can afford to fight this kind of battle, but I can't. I have a town to run. A family to protect and provide for. It's not worth it."

"Do you think Bob Whalen could be behind this smear campaign?"

He chuckled. "Bob and I are old friends. He'd never do anything to hurt me."

"Not even to win the nomination?"

"You make it sound like it's the White House or something. It's a party nomination for State Congress. Small potatoes. Not worth destroying a friendship. Not worth breaking up a marriage with untrue allegations. Not worth it. Carly, you're barking up the wrong tree."

"So it was because of the photo, though?"

"Yes. But that's between you and me."

Another deniable statement. The unspoken threat hung in the air between them.

She doubted she'd get him to change his story. "Thanks, Mayor. I should have the audit wrapped up in a day or so."

"Carly, your job is only to identify the monies taken, how they were accessed, and the possibility of their return. You were not hired to go all Jessica Fletcher on us and gather the suspects to identify the guilty party. Do you understand?"

Despite his snide reference to one of her favorite television programs, Carly figured she'd cut him some slack. After all, he was under a lot of pressure.

Like he said, a town to run. A family to protect and provide for. Ugly allegations and vicious rumors to overcome.

He had an uphill battle on his hands.

As did she. A murder to solve. A kidnapper to identify. A young boy's belongings to recover. Not to mention, a reason why somebody would try to run her husband off the road and frame him for drunk driving.

Her quiet little east coast town suddenly seemed not so quiet.

Or so safe.

$$$

Chief Donovan sighed. Seemed like he was doing a lot of that lately.

Every time Carly Turnquist called or visited, to be sure.

He picked up the phone. "Hello, Carly."

"Chief, you'll never guess what I just learned."

He sat back in his chair. This could be a long conversation. "Well, since I'll never guess, why don't we just cut to the chase and you tell me what you know."

"That would take a long time."

He wasn't catching her drift, but he couldn't let her know that. "Time I have."

Patience, not so much.

"I was doing some research on the Internet."

Ah, one of the new wonders of the twenty-first century. Not that it would ever replace good, old-fashioned police work. "And?"

"I discovered that both the mayor and Bob Whalen were running for State Congress."

"And?"

"The mayor withdrew from the race."

Probably happened a dozen times an electoral cycle, and nobody but Carly Turnquist would see a nefarious reason. He sighed. Again. "And?"

"Well, I called him. And he basically acknowledged it was because of that photo that the press got a hold of. And the allegations that he is having an affair with his secretary."

"Which, for anybody who knows Walt Akerman, knows that's completely out of character and untrue. I happen to be good friends with the family. My kids know his kids."

"Right. Well, I didn't say I believed the rumors."

"And not every rumor is true, which is what defines a rumor, isn't it? Which means not every rumor is a motive for murder. Or theft. Or conspiracy."

"Conspiracy? There's conspiracy going on?"

Oh, no. Had he opened another can of worms? "No. No conspiracy. At least, not so far as I know."

"Well, Chief, here's the thing. Bob Whalen has a bunch of people listed on his website. Who gave money to him for his campaign. But I don't know any of them."

"You aren't required to know them, Carly. He might know people you don't."

"True. But you'd think some of them would be names I'd recognize. From local politics. Regional businesses. That sort of thing."

"Possibly. But perhaps these are all too small for you to notice. Mom-and-pop shops, that kind of thing."

"I think you should check into Bob's financial records. Bank accounts, credit cards, that sort of thing."

"I don't know, Carly. That seems pretty intrusive. And we don't have any evidence that he's involved in anything other than running for Congress."

"True. He appears squeaky clean. But here's the thing, Chief. I was at his house the day Mike's car went off the road, and he said he couldn't talk to me right then because he was developing some photos in his dark room. But less than ten minutes later, he's up on the highway, first on scene at Mike's accident."

"Maybe he forgot something. An errand he had to run. Nothing criminal there."

"I thought the same thing. But get this. He drives a blue car."

"Lots of people drive blue cars."

"And there was blue paint on Mike's bumper."

He exhaled. Loudly. Hoping she'd get the hint. "We already talked about this. We don't know how long that was there."

"But Mike—"

"I know. Always walks around the car. Yada yada yada."

"Well, what about the fact Bob's car is blue?"

"So is mine, Carly. Does that make me a suspect?" When she hesitated, she shook his head. "I'm kidding." He pulled a notepad toward him and clicked a pen to ready it to write. "What do you want me to do?"

"Look at Bob's financials. See if his income as a paramedic supports his lifestyle. If not, where else is he getting money?"

"And if I don't find anything, will you leave this alone?"

"I think you will find something."

"But if I don't?"

"I won't bother you again."

The sweetest words he'd heard all day.

Chapter 16

What to have for lunch? Carly paced the kitchen, wishing somebody would show up at her door with lunch for four in hand.

Ding-dong.

She paused. Surely not. Nobody—and all those nobodys who sold food numbered one, the Dew Drop Inn—delivered in Bear Cove.

Carly gave up on lunch plans and headed for the front door. She peeked through the window. Chief Donovan. Holding a brown paper shopping bag.

Might still be lunch.

She opened the door. "If you're here to arrest me, I'm not going peaceably."

He smiled and removed his regulation cop hat. "No worries there. Thought it might be easier to show you than to explain it over the phone."

She stepped back. "An intriguing intro. Come in."

He entered and indicated the bag. "Thought you would be interested."

She patted her tummy. "If you tell me that bag contains sandwiches and hot coffee, I'll be more than interested. I'll do in my husband and marry you."

He chuckled. "The law might have something to say about that."

"As will your husband."

She whirled around and came face to face with Tom. "Ah, coming up for air?"

Her son quirked his chin toward the bag. "Couldn't let you eat all the food by yourself."

Chief Donovan headed for the kitchen. "No worries. The only food in this bag is food for thought."

Tom's mouth drooped. "Well, on that note, I'll head to the diner and get us some vittles. Any special requests?"

"That fish and chips was good."

He nodded. "On the condition that you'll still be here when I get back with it."

She tossed him a two-finger salute. "Aye, aye, Captain." A quick peck on the cheek. "You're more like your father every day. In looks and in attitude."

"Back in a jiff." He turned to the lawman. "Will you stay and eat with us?"

Donovan shook his head. "Thanks, but no. Got some other errands to run. Maybe next time."

Tom left, and Carly cleared a spot on the kitchen table. She gestured for the chief to sit, and he spread out his papers, shaking his head at her offer of coffee.

"I did what you suggested—"

She held up a hand.

"What?"

"I want to get a pen and paper and have you sign a statement to that effect."

"What effect?"

"That you did as I suggested. I've never had anybody say that before." She snapped her fingers. "Wait a minute. I think I have a tape recorder here. I'll get you to say that again. Then I'll put it on a repeating loop. Just to encourage me on those days when it seems like nobody listens to a word I say."

He shook his head, a slow smile creeping up his face. "Sit down and let me show you what I found."

She sat. "You can also make a note that I did as you suggested. First time. No argument."

He sifted through several pages. "I got a copy of Bob's bank statements, as well as a copy of Anita's." He pointed to several entries on both. "Here, and here."

She confirmed the amounts were the same. "Although, a thousand dollars isn't such an unusual amount. Lots of people withdraw or deposit in those amounts." She tapped the page. "I mean, it's not like he's paying her rent directly. Or her car payment. Stuff like that."

"But when we go back about a year, we see the exact same

pattern. And around the time the baby was born, he paid the Bear Cove Community Hospital directly."

"He would probably argue that was for his own care. Maybe he had an earache or something."

The chief shook his head. "I have the account number right here on the copy of this check."

She smiled. "Ah, the benefits of a good accounting system." She scanned the statements. "You know, some of these numbers look familiar." She rose and went to the folder in her office where she kept the town's financial records then returned to the kitchen. "Let's see. Right. A bit of a coincidence that the same day money goes missing from the town's account that it also pops into Bob's bank account. And from there to Anita's."

"Maybe a bit more than a coincidence." He pointed to another entry. "This is Bob's regular payroll amount. About what you'd expect—not round numbers. And the same with hers. Regular deposits from the hospital. Some a little more than others. Overtime, likely."

"I guess he might argue he sold some of his photography."

Chief Donovan shook his head. "He has a separate bank account for his business. And I checked into his tax returns. He files as single, a sole proprietor."

Carly narrowed her eyes. "Seems like you got your hands on a lot of information in a short period of time."

"I initiated search warrant requests. Wanted to do it all legal like. And the warrants were approved. But—"

"Will you be able to use this in court if needed?"

"Oh, sure. All I had to do was mention that I could get a warrant, and folks are happy to give over."

"So what next?"

"Next, we go visit the weak link in the chain. After you eat lunch. Remember your promise."

She smiled. "Anita."

$$$

"Anita."

The woman turned from the nurse's station, but when she saw Carly—or perhaps the chief of police who stood close at her side—her expression fell. "I'm busy."

The chief stepped forward. "I'm sure you are." He nodded at the other nurse behind the desk. "But I think Sadie will let you take your break now, won't you?"

Sadie, an older woman with bobbed reddish-blonde hair, nodded. "Sure. Take as long as you need."

Anita sighed. "Fine. The nurse's lounge is over here." She led the way into a cramped area no larger than a walk-in closet, then slumped in a worn vinyl chair. "What do you want?"

The chief nodded to Carly. On the ride over, they agreed to let her ask questions, feeling that perhaps a woman-to-woman talk would allow Anita to open up. The lawman would take over only if Anita wouldn't talk.

Carly drew a calming breath to settle the extra-large fish and chips churning in her stomach. "We need you to answer some questions about Bob and your relationship with him."

The woman tipped her head to one side. "What relationship?"

Carly leaned forward. Anita wasn't going to make this easy. "The one where you have a baby. The one where he pays you money every month."

Anita's shoulders slumped then her mouth drew in a hard line and she straightened. "You can't prove anything."

The chief tapped his folder. "Yes, we can. Enough for a judge and jury to ask some tough questions. Money going from him to you. On a regular basis. For the past year. Around the time you learned you were pregnant."

This time, her shoulders stayed slumped. "So Bob is the father of my child."

Nothing new there. Carly pressed in. "And he was paying you support?"

"It's what the courts would make him do if I took him to court. He knows it's his baby. And he wanted it kept on the hush-hush so his wife didn't find out."

Carly nodded. "Completely understandable." She sat back. "I've been in your spot, Anita. Loved a man who was completely unsuitable. Didn't end up pregnant, but I knew I couldn't have him."

Anita's eyes filled, and her bottom lip quivered. "I knew going into the relationship that he wouldn't leave his wife. She's the one with the money, although she keeps a tight hold on the purse strings. It's why he spends so much time taking pictures of birds. To earn a little extra to help me."

Carly met the chief's gaze. That might be Bob's story, but it was untrue. According to his business account, he barely sold enough photography to pay for his darkroom supplies. Three times in the past six months, he transferred money from his personal to his business account.

Anita wrung her hands together. "It's hard, being a single mother. Rent is high, daycare is expensive. I wanted him to support me so I didn't have to work. I had dreams of being a stay-at-home mom, but he said that's too much money. He'd have to work all the time to do that." A tear slipped down her cheek, gouging a rivulet in her makeup. "And he'll never leave her. If they divorce, he gets nothing. He signed a pre-nup."

That didn't seem like a smart choice to make. After all, if love was really involved, why the agreement? It was like predicting the end of the marriage before it started.

Perhaps Anita read her mind, because she tossed Carly a half-smile. "I wondered the same thing. I think at the beginning he really thought he loved her for herself, so the pre-nup didn't matter to him. But as time went by, she wore him down with her tight-fisted stranglehold on the family money."

Carly could see how that might affect a marriage relationship. Even though she'd never had that particular struggle. "Are you just going to settle for what you have with him?"

Another tear slipped down. "A part-time husband and father is better than none at all, don't you think? It's not like I have a lot of choices in a town this size."

Having been married to an abusive alcoholic, it felt like Anita was singing her song, and Carly swallowed past the lump forming in her throat. "I used to think the same thing. Until I realized that if I didn't leave, I couldn't expect anything different than what I already had."

Anita stared deep into her eyes, and Carly was certain the woman had reached the breaking point.

Then the nurse shook her head and sat back. "No, I'll stand by him. He stood by me. When I told him I was pregnant, I was so scared he'd insist I get rid of it. But he didn't. He said he'd work it out. And he has."

Carly nodded then turned to the chief. "I think you wanted to ask some questions, too?"

Their second pre-arranged signal.

He leaned forward, elbows on his knees. "The money that you take from Bob every month?"

"Support. For the baby."

"Given his family responsibilities, and his income, I dare say the courts would say he's paying too much."

She folded her arms across her chest. "It's what he wants to pay."

"I understand. But the courts might also think that because of his marital situation, he's paying you more than the law requires because he's afraid you might say something to his wife if he doesn't."

"I might have said that once or twice, but I didn't really mean it."

"And if he's paying you because he wants you to keep quiet, then that's blackmail."

The word hung between the three of them, and Carly held her breath. This was the telling moment, when Anita's motives—and her heart—would be revealed.

She looked from one to the other then back to the chief. "Just because I told him how much I needed doesn't mean I'd really go to his wife."

Chief Donovan kept his voice low. "The courts would see it differently."

She clasped her hands to her mouth, choking back a sob that slipped past her fingers despite her best attempts. "What will happen to us?"

Donovan kept his face impassive. If Carly didn't know better, she'd give him an Academy Award for his performance. "If you end up in jail, the baby will go to foster care. Get lost in the system. And even if you don't go to prison, Child and Family Services could remove him if they deemed you unfit as a parent."

A muffled gasp from Anita pulled at Carly's heart. The woman was torn between her child and her lover.

A terrible place to be.

Finally, Anita nodded and hung her head. "What do you need from me?"

Carly resumed her questions. "We believe Bob kidnapped my grandson."

"I don't know anything about kidnapping. He asked me to keep the kid at my place, since I live kind of out of town a bit, at the end of the road, near the park. Bob wanted to keep him in the shed, but that didn't seem right. I moved him into the house. Gave him a TV to watch. Fed him."

Carly shook her head. "Didn't you think that was strange?"

"He said the family was poor, didn't teach the kid how to behave in the house. Didn't want him keeping JW awake. I booked a couple of shifts off just to help him out." Anita looked up. "I'm in deep trouble, aren't I?"

"What else do you know?"

"Not much. I treated the boy right. Bob said he was watching him for a friend. But I thought that was strange, to keep him in a shed. Bob said he didn't want to put me out. But I took pity on him. Gave him books to read. Bob brought a bag with a telescope and a camera so the kid would have something to do. That's still in the shed. I was frantic when I saw the kid took off out through the window." She wrung her fingers together. "Actually, I was angry. It seemed he was being ungrateful, after all I did for him. But when I told Bob, he got so mad. Calling me names. Telling me I was stupid to move him into the house, that now he knew what both of us looked like." She stared at the floor. "I guess that's when I realized Bob wasn't telling me the whole truth."

You think? Love can make us so stupid.

"Did Bob say what his plans were for the boy?"

Anita swiped at the tears now freely running down her cheeks. "No. I kept asking him how long the kid was going to stay. But he wouldn't say. Kind of scared me. So in a way, I was relieved when the kid took off like that. I mean, maybe he'd forget where I lived. Kids that age get confused, don't they? Houses all look the same to them."

"So how did Bradley escape?"

Anita met her gaze straight on. "Escape? He didn't escape. I let him go."

$$$

Following Anita's startling revelation, the only thing Carly wanted to do was go home and cuddle with her husband.

But since he was still in the hospital, she did the next best thing.

She had the chief drop her there. He said he wanted to check in with the ER doc about Denver, and would gladly give her a ride home after her visit.

Given her abhorrence of exercise, she agreed to meet in the foyer in thirty minutes or so.

The walk down the hallway to his room at the rear of the building seemed shorter this time around. Maybe because she knew where she was going.

Or perhaps because she knew what to expect this time around.

Still, she was once again startled by the dark circles under his eyes. The blinds were closed, so she opened them a little to let in the sunshine.

He opened his eyes and smiled at her. "Now there's a sight for sore eyes."

She perched on the corner of the bed. "Are your eyes sore, too?"

He shifted in the bed, wincing at the movement. "No, just a figure of speech." He pursed his lips. "Got a kiss for me?"

She complied.

Happily.

And just to make sure he knew how much she missed him, she repeated it.

Now he was really smiling. "So, what's new with you?"

Where to begin? If she told him too much, he'd worry. But if she didn't tell him enough, he'd know she was holding back.

So she filled him in about Denver going missing and then being found again. And about her walk with Bradley. Her work on the town audit. The chief's connecting the missing money and Bob's bank account. And the revelation that Anita and Bob had a son together. She downplayed Anita's participation in Bradley's disappearance without actually saying she didn't know anything.

She didn't mention the threatening phone call. Or the fact Bob was an amateur photographer. Or the pre-nup.

She wasn't certain how all these things fit together yet, so could see no point in bringing anything into the story that might have no part in the ultimate solution.

At least, that's what she told herself.

As the old country song went, "that's her story and she's stickin' to it."

When she finished, she studied the various IV lines tethering her husband to his hospital bed. "Seems like there's a new one here." She indicated the additional bag hanging from the pole. "What's that for?"

"They think my blood pressure is up, so they're giving me something for it. Said it's a good thing I had the accident or I might never have known it was up. Said I'd need to stay in another day until it stabilizes."

She clutched his hand. "You never had a problem with your blood pressure before. Perhaps it's because of the accident? Your pain? Your desire to be home with your family? Your lost work time?"

He smiled. "I did try to explain that if I have high blood pressure, then I caught it from you."

She pouted and sputtered.

"They didn't buy it. Said that marriage actually decreases a person's normal pressure by ten points. I told them mine should increase since I'm married to you. The doctor agreed. Apparently he heard about you from Nurse Jones?"

"Not fair. Ganging up on me. Maybe I should just go home and heat up left over fish and chips and console myself."

"Now who's not being fair? They have me on a low sodium, low fat, low taste diet here." He pulled her close and snuzzled her hair. "Could you maybe smuggle in some of those leftovers?"

She wriggled out of his grasp. "Don't think so. Don't want you spending one second more here than necessary. I want you home tomorrow." She waggled a finger at him. "So you behave and do everything the staff tells you."

"Aye, aye, Captain." He laughed. "Usually you're the one saying that to me." He swatted at her hand. "Go home. Take care of our family."

"That's your job."

Bob's words echoed in her mind. Provide. Protect.

She missed Mike.

Chapter 17

What the chief didn't know wouldn't hurt him.

Or her.

At least, that's what Carly hoped.

So after she visited with Mike, she decided they needed to visit Anita again. She was fairly certain there was something more the woman hadn't shared. Perhaps if the law wasn't sitting across the table from her, she'd open up.

As she came out of Mike's room and made the turn toward the main entrance, Chief Donovan emerged from an office—the executive director of the hospital. Ross Bournes, a delightful man with a quick smile and a solid handshake. Which he proceeded to demonstrate.

If there was one thing she hated, it was men with limp fish grips.

She nodded and tossed him a smile. "Ross. Long time no see."

"Not since the last hospital fundraiser, I think. Two years?"

"At least." She acknowledged the chief's presence. "Chief."

The chief dipped his head. "How's Mike?"

"Not coming home today. Something about blood pressure."

Ross grinned. "Well, as we say in the health biz, high blood pressure is better than no blood pressure."

What was it with cops, morticians, and hospital folks? Some kind of gallows humor, she was sure. Occupational humor, for sure.

"Reminds me of a joke I heard the other day. Old accountants never die. They just lose their digits."

The two men stared at her, then Ross shrugged. "Must be something about their fingers falling off when they get old?"

Donovan peered at her. "Your fingers are going to fall off? Isn't that taking 'working your fingers to the bone' to the extreme?"

"Not fingers. Digits. You know, numbers? Accountants? Numbers?"

Donovan clapped Ross on the back. "I always think of accountants as boring bean counters, hey?"

"Well, totally necessary, of course." Ross lifted his mouth in a half-smile, half-apology. "Where would we be without accounting?"

Her thoughts exactly.

But not Chief Donovan's, apparently. "Oblivious to how bad off we really are? And know what? We wouldn't care. Only reason accountants survive is because of taxation. If the IRS didn't need to know how much to charge, we could all just do what we wanted and not worry about making a profit."

She sighed, having heard just about every anti-accountant argument on the planet. "But then we wouldn't know where to put more resources, and where to cut back, would we?"

Both Bournes and Donovan blinked at her. Did they expect—or need—an accounting lesson? When neither responded, she rolled her eyes at them. "For example, if you figured out it took a hundred dollars to feed a dog for a year, and a hundred dollars to feed a cow, which would you choose?"

Now it was Ross's turn to do the good-old-boy slap on the chief's back. "I'd feed the dog, of course. He's real good company, and he keeps strangers away. We can buy milk and hamburger at the supermarket."

Ha, ha, ha. Too funny.

Not.

The chief of police hitched at his duty belt. "Well, let's go, Ross." He turned to Carly. "Taking Ross here out for lunch."

Carly deliberated for a tiny moment about how much to say to him. Then she decided this was a case where asking for permission first was better than asking for forgiveness later. "I thought of a couple of more questions to ask Anita. I'll do that while you're at lunch, and maybe we can connect later?"

He peered at her through his bushy eyebrows for a moment, then nodded. "Sounds good. I'll be back in about an hour."

"Perfect."

She heaved a sigh of relief as the two men walked toward the staff entrance and the parking lot beyond.

An hour should be plenty of time.

$$$

Anita was just heading off duty when Carly rounded the corner to the surgery ward. The nurse looked none too pleased to see her for the second time that day, and indicated as much by leading the way to her car.

Carly trotted along beside her, keeping up a running commentary on the weather, the rain, the eclipse, and even the color of the awnings on the library entrance until they paused beside Anita's late model sedan.

Carly drew a couple of deep breaths to steady her breathing, leaning against the driver's door in case Anita tried to make a quick getaway.

But the nurse tossed her purse and kit bag into the back seat, then leaned against the rear bumper and lit a cigarette. After purposely blowing cigarette smoke in her direction—at least, that's how it seemed—Anita shrugged. "I know. Working in a hospital and smoking don't seem to go together." She flicked ash onto the asphalt then took another deep drag, exhaling through her nose. "Actually, I gave them up about four years ago. Haven't had even a single craving. Until this week."

"A lot of times that happens when we're under a lot of stress."

Anita snorted. "Stress. Yes, I guess that's one word for what's been going on." She narrowed her eyes at Carly. "What do you want now?"

"I had a few more questions."

"You're a real Columbo, aren't you? Always with the one more question routine."

Flattered she would be compared to another of her favorite television characters, Carly resisted preening. Instead, she tried the compassionate friend approach. A struggle for her, since she was neither naturally compassionate or a friend to Anita. "I'm sure it's been a difficult time. I married a father, and the kids were already teens, so I didn't have the struggle of raising them."

Anita shrugged. "Yeah, well, we make our choices."

"Has your family been supportive?"

A quick shake of the head. "Don't have family. Raised in foster care. Moved from place to place. Finally aged out from an orphanage."

"That must have been really difficult." There she went again, using the 'difficult' word. Did it sound as fake to Anita as it did to her own ears? She tried again. "I mean, moving to a new town, working full time, raising your son by yourself."

Anita smashed the cigarette butt under her toe. "Not really alone, though, am I? I mean, I have a part-time husband. When his wife goes out of town, he's all mine. Which is about one weekend a month. Almost like we share custody of the man. And I might see him a couple of evenings a week. For dinner. A quick liaison while our son naps. Always at his choosing. His convenience." Her mouth lifted in a wry smile. "If I sound bitter, it's because I am. Not at him. At her. She could divorce him tomorrow and we could be together. But no."

"Why not? Does she know about you?"

Another shrug. "I think she knows there's somebody in her husband's life, but I don't know if she knows who. I mean, a woman would know, wouldn't she? They haven't been—intimate for years. They sleep in separate rooms. But she won't divorce him because then she has to pay. Remember the pre-nup? Half a million bucks if she divorces him. His insurance, so to speak."

Hard to imagine a marriage based on insurance. But not everybody had the same chance at love she and Mike had. And despite both of them bringing some baggage into their marriage—he a widower, she a victim of abuse—they managed to work things through.

The only problem was, the picture Anita painted of Bob and Clarisse's marriage didn't match what she observed of their public lives. Of course, folks often put on an act so others didn't see the truth, but if that was the case, this was a very elaborate ruse.

Particularly since—but then again, Anita was likely getting only one side of the story.

Bob's.

Maybe knowing the truth would break down her walls of resistance and loyalty to a man who was obviously using her for his own ends.

Carly still hesitated, however, recalling something her mother often said: if you can't say something good, don't say anything at all.

Then again, this was about finding a murderer, a thief, and a kidnapper.

And with every passing minute, Carly was more certain one person played all three parts.

"I saw Clarisse last week, and she was looking very happy and healthy."

Anita lit another cigarette. "Don't talk to me about her. She's a witch with a capital B. She makes Bob's life a living hell."

"Have you met her?"

"About a year ago. In fact, the ironic thing is she introduced me to Bob." A humorless chuckle slipped out, along with a lungful of smoke. "At a library patrons picnic. From the first time I saw him, it was love at first sight. He said it was the same for him, too."

"But you haven't seen her since?"

"No. I am having an affair with her husband. Somehow it seemed tacky to socialize with her. Not that I move in her circles. Why?" Anita took a step closer, looming over Carly by several inches. "Is she dying of some rare, incurable disease?"

"Not that I know of."

The nurse leaned back against the car. "Too bad."

"No, I'd say that was very good. For her and for the baby."

The word hung in the air between them. Even Anita's cigarette seemed to have lost its attraction as it dangled between shaking fingers. The nurse closed her eyes and leaned her head back, taking several deep breaths before sinking to the ground beside her car. Her mouth crinkled into a grimace, then a sob escaped.

While sitting on the ground was the last thing she wanted—well, almost the last thing—Carly couldn't think of anything else to do. She glanced around. Nobody stirred. Nobody stared out through hospital windows.

She was it.

She settled beside the nurse and patted her arm. "I'm sorry."

Anita looked at her. "No, you're not. You're lying about the baby."

"Well, that would be easy to check out, wouldn't it?" Carly dug her cell phone from her purse. "Call Bob right now and ask him."

The woman stared at the phone as if it were a foreign object, then she shook her head. "No." She crushed the butt into the asphalt, seeming to take delight in twisting the filter until it disconnected from the shaft, sending bits of cottony fluff and tobacco leaves loose. "I wish I could do that to his face just about now."

"I had a husband I often thought about doing that to."

Anita looked up, her tears dried. "And did you?"

"No. He died before I had the chance." She held up one hand with her thumb and forefinger almost touching. "But I was this close."

"Maxwell Smart."

Another favorite of Carly's. Not as a role model, of course, but as a pressure reliever. "Right."

"Oh, what am I going to do?"

"You need to start thinking about yourself. And your baby."

Tears welled again. "I wanted to give him what I never had. A forever family."

"Maybe Bob's family will want to raise him."

Anita shook her head. "Unlikely. They're all about keeping up appearances. His wife won't want him. She'll have one of her own soon." She sobbed and leaned against Carly's shoulder. "I've made such a mess of things."

"Let me make a couple of quick phone calls. Maybe we can have a short term plans in place. And perhaps if you cooperate with the police, you could get a deferred sentence or something."

"Do you think so?"

Not really, but she could at least offer the woman a tiny glimmer of hope.

$$$

Carly met the chief when he returned to the hospital exactly twenty-nine minutes later. "Chief, we need to talk."

Ross waved them into a small board room. "Take all the time you need. See you later. Thanks for lunch."

The chief sat. "What's so all-fired important?"

"I chatted with Anita. Learned a lot."

Carly filled him in on their conversation in the parking lot about Bob's wife, his unborn baby, and Anita's concerns about her own child's care. "I told her I thought you might be able to put in a good word for her if she cooperated in the investigation."

He scowled. "She should have thought of that before. She's led us on a merry chase, avoiding telling us the whole truth, or even some of the truth, up until now."

"I called Tom. He and Sarah are approved by the State as foster parents. They took in Bradley when his father died. They said they'd be glad to take in Anita's baby if she is arrested."

The chief nodded slowly. "Sounds like a plan. What else did she tell you?"

"Once I explained that right now she's looking at conspiracy to kidnap because she helped Bob take Bradley, and that's a big prison sentence, she caved. Told me she helped Bob because of the baby. They're in love. Bob told her Mike's accident was just that, but once he came on the scene, he wanted to discredit Mike and distract me, so he splashed the alcohol around to make it look like he was driving drunk. Said he tried to force alcohol down Mike's throat but you guys got there too soon. Which is why there was none in his system."

"Do you believe her?"

Carly shook her head. "No. There's the paint on the rear bumper. The fact Bob was there at all points to this being more than a simple happenstance. I don't think he set out that day to harm Mike specifically, so the hit-and-run was more a crime of opportunity. But Denver said he heard two bangs. Which indicates that when one didn't work, he hit the car again, driving it into the guardrail and hopefully over the edge. Just like I don't think he went to the park intending to kill Paulson. The rock points to the fact he didn't premeditate and bring a weapon. But I think Bob would tell her what he figured she wanted to hear to satisfy her. Love has a strange way of plugging our ears and deafening our logic."

He chuckled. "Sounds like you've got it all figured out."

"I think we need to pay Bob a visit. Before Anita gets scared or convinced she isn't in trouble and talks to him."

"Speaking of which, where is she?"

"At home, getting the baby's stuff together so Tom and Sarah can pick him up. She said she'll write the court a letter asking them to appoint the kids as temporary guardians in her absence. That makes it easier. I don't want to see the child spend even one night in foster care."

"Do you think she can be trusted?"

"Right now, she's so hurt by Bob's betrayal of their relationship, and his lies, that she'll do whatever you ask. But that might not last forever, particularly if he contacts her."

Chief Donovan stood. "Then let's get over to Bob's right away. And I hope you're right. About Anita, and her willingness to work with us."

Carly hoped so, too.

Without that, three lives stood to be irreparably damaged.

$$$

The man is a bold-faced liar!

Whatever Carly thought Bob Whalen would say, it certainly wasn't this.

From the time they arrived at Bob's house, things went from bad to worse. First, he wouldn't let them in, so they held their conversation on the front landing. With Bob standing on the top step, the chief on the second, and Carly on the pathway leading to the driveway.

A psychological gambit she often sought to exploit—give an impression of authority from a higher physical position—was now being used against her.

And based on the relaxed shoulders, half-grin, sarcastic tone, and condescending manner, Bob Whalen had this particular ploy down pat.

"No, Chief, I don't know what you're talking about. Sure, Anita and I had some good times. But her allegations are unfounded and untrue." He leaned in closer to the lawman as though to share a confidence. "Actually, I broke off with her just yesterday." He straightened and looked Carly right in the eye. "I realized how unfair I was being to my wife and family. So I confessed to them last night. It was hard. And my wife is still very angry at me. She won't return to our home for a while. But we are still very much in love. And very married. And we intend to welcome our unborn child into our solid marriage and united family."

The chief tried another tack. "So you deny you stole money from the town to pay Anita support and to keep your affair a secret?"

Bob's eyes widened. "Did Anita tell you that?" He stomped a foot. "I had no idea the woman could be so vindictive. No, I lent her money when she needed it."

"Every month?"

"Yes, Carly, every month, as it so happens. Seemed she wasn't very good with finances. Always some sort of an emergency. Tires for her car. The kid was sick. Lost days at work. Women's things." He nudged the lawman. "You know how women can be. Always pulling at your heartstrings."

The chief shot her a look. "And what about Bradley?"

"The kid?" He shrugged. "She got all hysterical when he saw me kissing her good-bye one morning. She said she'd tell my wife if I didn't grab the kid to keep him quiet until she could come up with a plan. At that point, honestly, I just wanted to be rid of her, so I went along. And I didn't kidnap him. I told him I had some cool pictures and he came with me happily. Spent his time going through albums, watching home movies, eating junk food. You know how kids are. They'll make up stories just to tell you what you want to hear and to stay out of trouble."

Kind of like you're doing right now.

Carly gritted her teeth. "Bradley doesn't tell lies."

"No?" Bob tipped his head to one side. "Never?"

He had a point.

The chief nodded and replaced his hat. "Well, thanks, Bob. That's it for now." He turned toward the cruiser they arrived in. "But don't make any plans to leave town. I might have more questions."

"You know where I live, Chief. But please keep your bulldog there on a short leash. She scares me."

Carly stepped forward to respond but the chief gripped her by the forearm. "Not now."

He held open the passenger front door and she slid in, pushing aside the empty disposable coffee cups to make room for her feet. Then he closed the door, rounded the vehicle, and slid into the driver's seat. "I know. He's lying through his teeth. But we don't have enough evidence to arrest him. He'll make a mistake, and then we'll get him."

She folded her arms across her chest. "But Anita's own words mean you'll arrest her, right?"

He nodded. "I'll drop you home, then head over there. You might tell Tom to be ready to take the kid tonight."

A knot formed in her throat. "Doesn't seem fair."

"It's not. But it's the law."

Chapter 18

"Chief, one more thing."

Donovan sighed. Seemed that with Carly, there was always one more thing. "Yes?"

"About Denver."

"What about him?"

"I don't think that's his real name, do you?"

"Probably not." He leaned against the door jamb at the station, scratching that spot in his back that always tickled when more work was in the process of being heaped upon him. "But does it matter?"

As he suspected, she wasn't going to let the matter drop. "I wondered if we might take a look at missing persons records. See if he has family who are looking for him?"

He sighed. "We're right in the middle of a huge investigation here. Sure, Anita is under lock and key, and thanks, by the way, for suggesting your son as foster care for her little one. They sure seemed to be getting along great."

The image of the infant staring up at Sarah Turnquist as she cuddled him brought a hitch in his throat. The little one looked like he naturally belonged there.

Carly waved off his words like a pesky fly. "Sure, sure. She loves babies. And Bradley is thrilled to have a little brother. Even though we explained he might only be visiting for a while."

"Unless we get more evidence on Bob Whalen, Anita could be

looking at a long stretch in state prison. And even if she does turn state's evidence, there's no guarantees."

"But what about Denver? He's still a material witness."

"An inconsistent one at best, unreliable at worst. I can see him now, on the witness stand. A good defense attorney would tear him—and his testimony—to shreds."

"But if we could prove he has ties to the community—"

"What ties? He's a transient. Homeless, technically. Nobody around here knows him or can vouch for him."

She shoved her hands into her pants pockets. "Sit me at a desk and show me how to do some searches. Let me see if we can find somebody connected to him."

Donovan exhaled. "Fine. Over here."

He led the way to an extra desk and computer, and spent a few minutes showing her the missing persons database. "You can put in physical characteristics, such as height, hair and eye color, gender. That narrows the field. Oh, and age, too, although we don't know his exact date of birth."

She tapped on the keyboard. "Male. Brown hair. Brown eyes. I'd say he's thirty-five to forty years old." She closed her eyes. "What else?"

"Didn't notice any scars."

She looked up at him. "No, but he did say he liked working with wood. So I can put that here under skills, right?" She typed in a couple of words, then hit enter. "Oh, dear. More than six hundred hits."

"You need to narrow your search."

"Okay. He said he stopped drinking four years ago. So I'd say he was probably not homeless when that happened. So let's put in missing less than a year. He's in very good condition, and he is well-educated, so I think if somebody was looking for him very long, they'd have found him by now."

"If anybody is looking. Not everybody has a loving family or a strong network of friends, you know."

"Sad but true. When Mike's brother Jerry was missing all those years, occasionally Mike talked about looking for him. I think after the first few times when he found him but his brother really didn't want help, Mike kind of gave up. Some people just march to a different drummer, don't they?"

He chuckled. She headed up her very own category of peculiar people, and she didn't even know it. "Some people like living without any accountability."

"But they know where to go when they decide to do things differently. Jerry did. He tracked Mike down and showed up on our doorstep with Bradley in tow."

She hit enter, and this time fourteen names filled the screen. He pointed to a couple. "Some have pictures. Some only have a sketch. Or an old picture. You can click here," he indicated a tab on the screen, "and it opens each case individually."

"I'll work my way down through these and see if I come up with something."

"Fine. I can let you do that because I officially deputized you. But please don't poke around into any other areas. Focus on finding out who Denver is."

"Right."

She stared at the screen, using the mouse to navigate from one page to another.

Seemed safe enough to leave her on her own.

Then again, with Carly, could he ever be certain?

$$$

An hour later, and a familiar face materialized on the screen. Carly gasped. A much-younger, well-groomed marine stared back at her, eyes somber with a hint of a smile hiding beneath the standard military portrait.

Denver.

No, not Denver.

Ryan Hamilton.

From, of all places, Denver, Ohio. Hence the moniker he adopted in his new life.

She studied his story. Career-bound military man. Served numerous tours. Desert Storm veteran. Special Ops assignments. Medical discharge two years prior for PTSD. Disappeared sixteen months ago. Went out for a walk and never returned. Family frantically searching for him. Wife and nine-year-old son.

Interesting. Maybe that's why he seemed to get along with Bradley so well. The two boys were around the same age. Had Denver's memories caught up with him? Is that why he changed when talking to her grandson?

Or did something else happen?

Had Paulson acted aggressively toward him, and Denver—Ryan—reacted instinctively and killed him? Or perhaps the journalist reminded him of someone from his past? Did Denver know exactly who he was but didn't want to return to his former life?

Perhaps abandonment by an abusive husband and father was better for his wife and son than if he remained and continued mistreating them.

Then again, if his wife didn't want him found, why report him missing? Unless there was money involved.

She didn't know much about PTSD, so after she printed the case file, she exited to the search engine and typed in the acronym. Thousands of hits listed for the syndrome, and she scanned several articles, looking for common factors and symptoms.

Seemed PTSD could be caused by any number of events, from childhood trauma to what used to be called battle fatigue. And the symptoms were many and varied: panic attacks, nightmares, addictions, violence, schizophrenia and other mental illnesses, or simply an inability to cope with everyday life events such as personal hygiene or handling money wisely.

She focused on a website from the Department of Veterans Affairs, which spoke about the impact on serving and retired military, as well as their families, their careers, and their social relationships.

By the time she finished, her head swam with facts and figures, but no perfect answers. She rose and headed for the chief's office, tapping on the door before entering. She handed him the case file she'd printed out. "I'm pretty sure this is him. It's an older picture, but it looks—and sounds—like Denver."

Chief Donovan scanned the page and nodded. "Good work. Appears his wife and kid will be happy to know he's safe. Want to call them?"

"I'd rather check in with Denver first. Make certain he wants to be found. If he doesn't, he's likely to disappear again, and with him, the evidence we need to identify our suspect."

"True. Why don't you do that?"

"I think I'll ask the pastor to break the news to him. They get along well, and I don't think Denver really likes me."

"I wouldn't hold it against him. Deep down somewhere, he probably knows he's got a secret. Maybe his memory just wouldn't let it surface."

She nodded. "From what I was reading, something as simple as an argument with a spouse can be enough to set someone with PTSD off. It's like the fight-or-flight mechanism in their brain is set extremely low, so it doesn't take much and they want to run."

She returned to the desk and made the call to the pastor, who assured her he'd talk to Denver and see what he wanted. She gave him the contact information for Denver's wife, and hung up.

All in all, a good day. Yes, Anita was in jail and her son officially in the foster care system, but the child was in the best of hands. Plus she was close to reuniting Denver with people who loved him.

Now to find enough evidence so the chief could arrest her suspect.

$$$

Carly snuggled next to Mike on his hospital bed. "I don't know how you can sleep in this plastic bed."

Mike chuckled. "Oh, it's not so bad once you get used to it."

"But it crinkles and crackles every time I move."

"That's the mattress cover."

"I know what it is, and it grosses me out." She sighed and flexed her toes. "Nothing like our good old bed at home."

He wrapped an arm around her. "I should be getting out later today." He buried his face in her hair. "Although, if they came in here right now and took my blood pressure, they'd probably keep me in for another week."

She laughed. "No way am I letting them get away with that. You need to get home so you can spend some time with the kids." She sat up. "Speaking of which, have they been to visit?"

"Couple of time every day, morning and night. Came in earlier with the wee one in her arms. That was a surprise." He pulled her back beside him. "I'm glad you thought to put in a good word for them."

"I'm glad they were open to the idea. It was kind of short notice."

"Sarah loves babies. Surprised they don't have one of their own yet."

She laughed again. "Give them some time. They got married and had a son before the honeymoon was over, remember."

"I do remember. I was there, too."

She thought back to the wedding that almost didn't happen. "I think they didn't want to take on too much at once, what with their careers and such. Plus, I know they wanted to spend more time with Bradley, getting to know him, helping him through all the changes in his life, before adding babies to the mix."

Mike smiled. "He sure has settled in, hasn't he?"

Yes, he had.

And her husband was looking better every minute, it seemed. Or maybe she missed him so much that she overlooked the bruises on his arms. But today the IV's were removed, and he said he ate breakfast on his own. Went to the bathroom once with assistance and now enjoyed going by himself. All good signs.

Voices in the hallway drew her attention, and she sat up again. If Nurse Jones caught her—

A neatly-dressed man appeared in the doorway. He hesitated and smiled at them.

Carly stared.

An older version of the marine's photo in the missing person's file.

She slid from the bed and crossed the room. "Denver?"

He nodded. "Yes, ma'am." He rubbed his chin. "Didn't know if you'd recognize me. Shaved off the beard and got the hair cut."

She smiled up at him. "It takes years off you." She gestured to the easy chair beside Mike's bed. "Come on in."

"Thank you." He nodded to Mike. "Sir."

Mike shook his head. "Makes me feel old when folks call me sir. Sit."

Denver complied and Carly returned to her spot on Mike's bed, her feet dangling.

Denver cleared his throat. "Wanted to come and say thank you for everything you did."

Carly started to speak, but Mike nudged her with his foot. She closed her mouth and smiled at the man.

Denver continued. "The pastor called and talked to me. When he told me about my wife, I remembered. Everything. Then he asked if I wanted to go home. And I said yes."

Carly wrung her hands together. "Oh, that's so good to hear."

He nodded. "I see now that I've been looking for home and family for the past months."

Mike shifted in the bed. "Do you want to talk about it?"

Denver crossed one leg over the other. "My wife wanted me to enroll in therapy, and I thought I had it under control. That's why we argued. And something in me snapped. I left the house, trying to walk off my frustration. I think I got mugged, because I had a wallet, a cell phone, keys, and money. The next thing I remember is waking up in the Greyhound station in Augusta, with only the clothes on my back."

This was terrible. The poor man. "And no memories?"

"Nothing. Except Denver. I thought it was my name. I figured that whatever came before must be so bad—or I must be so bad—

the only way to go was forward."

Mike smiled. "So what's next?"

"My wife and son are on their way here. They should arrive later today. The pastor is putting them up at his house until we figure out what's next. She says she wants me to come back home. That my boy misses me." He dropped his head. "I don't know that I deserve them, but that's what she says."

A second chance. What great news. "I hope you'll plan to come to our home for dinner. Maybe tomorrow?"

"That sounds swell. I think my son Tony would get along great with Bradley." He stood. "Well, I just wanted to thank you for all you've done."

More voices in the hallway alerted them to additional visitors. Mike chuckled. "It's like Grand Central Station here today."

Mayor Akerman paused outside the door and poked his head in. "Oh, you've got visitors. We can come back later."

Mike waved them in. "Come on in. Lots of room."

The mayor stepped back, spoke to someone, then entered. He crossed the room and perched on the window ledge. "Just for a couple of minutes. Ran into Chief Donovan in the hallway, and he said you were still here, Mike. Wanted to see how you're doing." He nodded at Carly, who returned the greeting, then turned to Denver. "Don't think we've met."

Another man entered the room and stood behind the mayor and to one side with the chief close behind. Denver's expression changed, and he pointed. "That's the man who was there when Mike had his accident. The man I saw splashing alcohol around."

Chapter 19

Carly stared. What? The mayor? While she hadn't completely ruled out the possibility that he hired her as a cover-up for taking the funds, she'd never seriously considered him a suspect.

And while Bob denied any part in the accident, Anita as much as said he'd confessed to her. Unless she was lying. If so, was everything she said a lie?

And if the mayor had run Mike off the road, what was his motive?

Chief Donovan stepped forward and clamped a hand on the mayor's arm while tossing her a look that mirrored her own confusion.

She shrugged and turned back to Denver. "Are you sure?"

Denver nodded. "Positive. Told you I'd know him if I saw him again, even though I couldn't describe all the parts."

The mayor frowned and shrugged off the chief's grip. "Let go of me."

Chief Donovan reattached himself to the man's arm. "Walter Akerman, you're under arrest for—"

Denver stepped forward. "No, not *him*." He looked past the mayor to the man standing behind him. "Him."

The mayor took a step to the left, revealing Bob Whalen, who lifted his hands, palms up. "And you want to believe this crazy homeless man who wanders around the woods?"

Carly turned to Denver. "Have you ever met this man?"

"No."

"Where did you see him before?"

"At Mike's accident. And then later in the woods. The day that newspaper guy died."

Bob folded his arms over his chest and grinned. "See, like I said. A crazy guy in the woods."

Carly peered at him. "Is that how you knew he was in the woods? Because you were there too? To meet Harvey Paulson?"

Bob took a step back. "No." He glanced around, but the chief and the mayor blocked his only exit. He straightened his shoulders. "So what if I was? No law against me being in the park."

The chief released the mayor and edged closer to Bob. "There is if you're involved in blackmail. And murder." He slipped his handcuffs off his duty belt. "Are you going to come quietly, or do we need these?"

Bob glared at Carly. "Fine. Have it your way. I didn't know what I was going to do, but when I saw Mike ahead of me on the road, I saw it as the perfect opportunity to distract you from the town audit. Thought if I could fill up your time with defending your reputation and your husband's, you'd stop investigating."

She nodded. Although things didn't quite fit exactly into place. Not yet, anyway. "It's about running for congress, isn't it?"

Bob's cheeks colored and he glanced at the mayor. "Sorry, Walt. Yeah, I knew I didn't stand a chance of defeating the mayor. He already had political and administrative experience. All I had were a bunch of good ideas and some promises. Plus, I'd never get elected if there was even a hint of scandal. So long as you were looking into the missing money, that shadow would hang over me. Plus the thing with Anita."

The *thing* with Anita that involved a woman's broken heart, her ruined reputation, and an innocent child.

Mike sat up straighter in the bed. "What about the photos of the mayor and his secretary?"

"Yeah, that was me, too. I doctored a couple of photos and sent them anonymously to the media."

Carly recalled the journalist's words. "And the money?"

Bob threw his hands in the air. "Fine. I promised the stations and the paper that I'd spend a lot of election dollars if they carried the story. At first, they didn't want to but that helped change their minds."

One question answered. Only about a hundred more to go.

"Where were you planning to get the money to keep that promise? We all know elections are won or lost in the media."

He lifted his chin and glared at her. "My wife is very supportive of my run for Congress."

No doubt imagining herself a part of the *nouveau* royalty—American politicians and their wives. Shades of Jackie Kennedy, perhaps?

"Why kidnap Bradley?"

He hesitated a moment as though he would deny the allegation, then his shoulders slumped. "He saw us kissing. I was afraid he'd tell somebody and my wife would find out. I just needed him out of the way for a few days. Until I had enough money from outside backers that I didn't need hers."

"Thought you just said your wife was very supportive."

His cheeks colored a deeper shade of red. "Well, yes, but—"

"But the backers didn't come through." Carly knew because of the lack of financial supporters listed on the website. "Did they?"

"You think you know everything, don't you?"

"Not everything, but one thing I do know for certain."

Another glare. If looks could kill... "What's that?"

"My faith in the media has been restored."

Mike slapped the bed. "What? They tried to paint you as a loony."

She grinned. "But they didn't succeed. I'm not as crazy as they let on."

$$$

At dinner that evening, Carly surveyed the people gathered around her table. Mike, recently released from hospital, sat in his usual place, to her left. She gripped his hand yet again, and he tossed her a genuine but tired smile. As soon as dinner was done, she'd see him to bed.

Across from her, Tom and Sarah, along with Bradley. Anita's baby, JW—which, they'd since learned, stood for John Whalen—slept in his bassinet in Bradley's room. Sarah bloomed with new-mother radiance, and Carly suspected it wouldn't be long before they announced the impending arrival of a baby of their own. Bradley, sitting between his parents, dug into his dinner with an enthusiasm born of happiness rather than appetite.

Finally, his family was back together again. With a baby brother—albeit temporary, perhaps—to boot.

And at the end opposite from Mike, Chief Donovan. With no wife at home, and the way his face lit up at the offer of a home cooked meal, Carly took pity on him and included him in their celebration.

They spent enough time together over the past few days to qualify as near-family, at least.

And while not fancy, the takeout from the Dew Drop Inn was exactly what everybody wanted.

Although this time around, Bradley was wise enough not to order an extra-large extra-special fish and chips *and* a side of wings.

Not so Carly. She dug into her soggy fries drowned in peas, stuffing, and gravy. A gravy-laden pea missed her mouth and dropped into her lap. "Rats. A clean shirt bites the dust."

Mike smiled from behind his coffee cup. "Maybe we need to get you a bib."

She raised her eyebrows. "Oh, like the one you wore in hospital?"

His cheeks pinkened. "Shirt saver, not bib, I'll have you know."

She studied the gravy stain on her jeans. "Shirt saver. Might have to get me some of those." She glanced at Bradley. "What do you think? Pink or purple?"

He glanced at his parents then grinned at her. "Red plaid flannel."

She reached across the table for him but he sat back in his chair, just out of reach. As well he knew. "Just because we live in Maine doesn't mean we always wear plaid flannel."

Bradley used his fork to count off on his fingers. "Let's see. Nightgown. Garden jacket. Housecoat. Slippers." He looked toward the cat bed in the corner. "Doc's bed."

She tossed her napkin at him. "Okay. Fine. I get the hint."

He tipped his head in question. "You're going to buy something other than plaid flannel?"

"No, silly. I'm going to outfit you completely in blue plaid flannel when we go shopping tomorrow."

The adults joined Carly in laughing as Bradley's cheeks reddened.

It was good to hear.

Chapter 20

One thing still bothered Carly. Well, if she had to admit it to herself, more than one thing—life was never that simple, was it?—but one final detail she *had* to know the answer to. She planted her elbows on the table and addressed the police chief. "Chief, what about the picture Harvey Paulson clutched in his hand?"

He shook his head. "Haven't figured that one out, yet."

Sitting beside the lawman, Tom chuckled. "Oh no, not an unsolved mystery. How will you ever sleep?"

She jabbed a foot in his direction under the table, but he pulled out of reach. "Stop teasing. You know how I like to have everything tidied up."

Mike nodded. "Just like your files and your desk. Can't bear to leave a single detail out of place."

She ginned at her husband. "Unlike your vertical filing system."

"I rarely lose anything."

She jabbed a finger in his bicep. "Only because you're smart enough not to go looking for it." She tossed a smile at Sarah. "If he sets just one thing on top of another, he can't find the first thing."

Her daughter-in-love shook her head. "I don't know how you stand it, but at least now I understand where Tom gets his concept of orderly disorder from."

Carly held her hands in a gesture of surrender. "It was already ingrained in him before I entered the picture. I tried to change him, but it was too late."

Laughter erupted around the table. Even Bradley, who looked from one to the other as though seeking an explanation, joined in. Carly had a pretty good idea he didn't have a clue what the joke was about, but it didn't matter.

They were all family. They were together. The killer was in jail. The baby was asleep.

Almost everything was right with her world.

Almost.

And until everything was, she wouldn't let it go. "It seemed funny that Paulson would be carrying around an older photo of the mayor. We know he didn't go there to meet Akerman."

Donovan dabbed at his lips with his napkin then dropped the linen square into his lap. "Right. The mayor has an air-tight alibi."

Mike leaned forward. "But you did suspect him at some point, didn't you?"

Carly nodded. "Almost everybody in town was a suspect at one time or another. The only thing I knew for sure was that I didn't take the money."

Mike's smile fell away. "And me. You didn't thing I could have taken it, right?"

Ah, the chance to throw her husband's cool demeanor for a loop. "Well. . ."

His eyebrows raised. "Really?"

She laughed. "No, not really. So only three hundred and ninety-eight other suspects. Not to mention all the people who came into town for the eclipse. Imagine the stress of having to check out all those alibis." She glanced at the chief. "I never really appreciated how difficult your job could be."

He nodded. "And it's always made more difficult because people lie to us. Or they don't tell us the whole truth. Or they try to avoid talking to us at all."

Bradley tapped the lawman's forearm. "Maybe they're just shy, Chief Donovan."

Another nod. "Or scared."

"My dad says I shouldn't be scared of the police. They're my friend."

Donovan smiled. "I sure hope so, Bradley."

Carly sipped her coffee, enjoying the conversation and the companionship. But after a few minutes, her thoughts strayed back to the dead journalist. Who was he meeting in the woods? And why was the photo so important?

As she contemplated these questions, the telephone rang. She sighed and set her cup down. "I'll get it." She crossed to the counter and picked up the handset. "Hello."

"Carly, this is Joe down at the newspaper."

"Thanks for the tip about following the money."

"Sure. Any time. Got another for you."

"I'm all ears."

"Just went down to the photo archive to do some research, and I saw something I think you might be interested in."

"I don't know, Joe." She turned her back to the table and glanced over her shoulder. "Mike probably doesn't want me getting involved in anything else for a while. He just got out of the hospital today."

"Well, it's not a new mystery. Just thought maybe you were looking for answers to some questions. But never mind."

She braced the phone between her ear and her shoulder. "You can't leave me hanging now, Joe. Spill."

He chuckled. "Well, like I said, I was down in Archives and saw the photo log. That journalist that died?"

"Paulson."

"Right. Well, he checked out a stock photo of the mayor from the archives. And one of his secretary. Two separate images. Don't know if that means anything to you, but thought I'd share it. Talk to you later."

Carly replaced the handset and returned to her chair. The others chattered good-naturedly. Any worries she had about Mike overhearing the conversation vanished. He was much too busy—and perhaps even too tired—to pay attention to her right now.

Which was good for her.

Because despite Joe's intentions, his information achieved the opposite effect.

Instead of answering her question, instead it opened a whole new can of worms.

$$$

Thankfully, right after dinner, Mike excused himself to go lie down. Tom and Bradley volunteered to do the clean-up, and Sarah relaxed in her room, leaving Carly and the chief free to follow-up on Joe's phone call.

Once presented with the opportunity, she didn't hesitate. "Chief, we need to talk to Bob." She quirked her chin toward the telephone. "I'll fill you in on the way."

He nodded and headed for the car, while Carly told Tom she was going out for a few minutes.

He wasn't exactly happy, but seeing as how he couldn't talk her out of it, he nodded. "At least you'll be with the chief. I mean, how much trouble can you get in while you're with the law?"

She tossed him what she hoped was a reassuring grin, then left. Within a couple of minutes, she strode into the jail with the chief close on her heels. She tapped her toe on the floor while he unlocked the door to the cells. "Should we play this good cop, bad cop?"

He peered at her. "And which am I?"

She smiled. "Maybe we'll just see how it goes."

He nodded. "From what you told me, that sounds like a good plan. You're pretty sure what he's going to say, aren't you?"

She nodded. "Unfortunately, I think so. It seems that the more times I get involved in investigations, the more I start to think like the bad guys."

"Well, that's what makes us different than them, you know."

"What's that?"

"We might think like them, but we don't act like them."

His words reassured her in a strange way. Just because she understood why a person made bad choices didn't mean that was her destiny.

Bob lounged on the cot in his cell. He swung his feet to the floor and sat up, leaning against the wall. His pulled-down brow indicated his displeasure with their presence.

Or perhaps just hers.

The chief nodded to the prisoner. "We had a couple of questions for you."

Bob looked past them. "Where's my lawyer?"

"Do you want him?"

"Do I need him?"

"No."

The man clasped his hands behind his head. "Fire away."

"Wanted to ask about the picture Harvey Paulson had in his hand."

Bob's mouth lifted in a half-smirk. "Then maybe you should ask him." He snapped his fingers. "Oh, sorry. He's dead." He peered at them. "What difference does the picture make at this point?"

"Just wrapping up a few loose ends."

Bob stood and crossed the cell in two strides, standing almost nose to nose with them. He jerked his head in Carly's direction. "You mean, she wants to know, right?"

Carly exhaled. Was he always this big a jerk? Or had jail time changed him already? "Maybe I'll tell you what I think, and you can confirm or deny it." She smiled her sweetest smile. "Will that work better for you?"

Bob shrugged. "We can give it a try."

"Harvey Paulson originally came to Bear Cove to follow the lunar eclipse story. We met him at the bus station, and he was interviewing folks in town for a personal interest piece."

"How interesting. Not." Bob feigned a yawn. "The intricacies of the media."

Refusing to allow his off-putting attitude to distract her, she continued. "He saw the news article about the mayor and his secretary. So he decided to change the focus of his story. Look into small time politics in small towns, or something like that. He went to the newspaper archive and asked for some stock photos of the mayor and his secretary. And when he saw them, he realized what you'd done."

Bob's eyes widened, and his mouth formed an "o", but the half-smirk lingered below the surface.

She ignored him again. "As a photo-journalist, he knew you altered the photos, removing the mayor's wife from one and inserting Evie instead. He could have done the same research I did, where I learned about your photography skills." She peered at him. "Were you trying to force Akerman to withdraw from the congressional race? I think you knew you didn't stand a chance of beating him, and you needed to win. Desperately. Your wife was willing to fund your campaign, but she wouldn't fund your mistress. I suspect you were skimming money off the top, setting it aside in a little nest egg for yourself. Did Anita know you planned to leave her when you had enough to satisfy you?"

He shrugged then sauntered back to his cot, stretching out as though ready for a nap. "I don't know what she knows. I don't care. I really was looking for a way to end it. But every time I said I thought we should cool it for a while, she'd get all crying and threatening to tell my wife."

Despite Bob's willingness to be so forthcoming, there was still another question Carly had for him. "Did you really think you'd scare me off with that phone call?"

Bob rested his shoulders against the wall. "No harm in trying, I figure." He studied her from the corner of his eye. "Got to admit, you were a tougher bird than I expected."

The chief cleared his throat. "So what happened? Paulson contact you, threaten to tell what he knew?"

"I thought I could buy him off." Bob chuckled. "Imagine. An honest reporter. Who'd'a thought?"

Carly shook her head. "What's even more ironic is that you, as a future representative of the people, should be upset because someone else couldn't be bought."

"Ironic, isn't it?"

"No, Bob, it's not ironic. It's sad."

$$$

One more stop before she headed home.

Anita was housed in the opposite end of the cells from Bob, out of sight, where he couldn't harass or intimidate her. Carly stopped outside the cell.

Anita looked up from a magazine she thumbed through. "How is JW?"

"He's doing fine. Tom and Sarah love him like their—m" She paused. Hearing that her child was fitting in so well likely wouldn't be the comfort words she wanted to hear. Perhaps stretching the truth a little and saying he was fussing because he missed his mother—no, she wouldn't lie. Better not to say anything. "I wanted to ask another question, if you're up to it."

Anita nodded. "My arms ache to hold him, you know?" She sighed. "What did you want to know?"

"You said you let Bradley escape. Were you just saying that?"

She shook her head. "I was starting to question some of the things Bob was telling me. Saying he thought we should not see each other for a while until everything cooled off around town. Suggesting his wife knew about us and he didn't want to lose her financial backing before the election. Stuff like that." She exhaled with a shudder. "Honestly, once I figured out he was probably the one who killed the journalist, I got scared. I thought maybe he'd do something like that if I caused him any trouble."

Carly nodded. "A deadly dissolution." When Anita tipped her head in question, Carly explained. "A dissolution is an accounting term for when a business arrangement, like a partnership, is dissolved. Sometimes it's amicable. More often it's not."

Anita exhaled. "I didn't know the term, but I understood the potential. Anyway, I didn't think it was right to keep the boy locked in the room. So when I brought in a tray with food on it, I also put a table knife there. I guess I hoped he was bright enough to use it to cut his way out somehow. Isn't that what all those superheroes the kids adore these days do?"

Superheroes. Yes, what she said made perfect sense. For her, MacGyver was one of those guys who could take chewing gum and baling wire and make whatever he needed. And Bradley was a smart kid. A table knife would certainly work as the tool he needed to remove a screw from a windowsill and then to cut out a screen.

If only all of life's problems could be solved so easily.

$$$

As Carly and the chief pulled into the driveway, another thought occurred to her. "Wonder why he didn't take the photo? If he had, we might never have known about Bob's involvement in the fake news article."

The chief shook his head. "Maybe Paulson didn't show him the photo. Most likely he'd have held that part back. Wouldn't make sense to show Bob the evidence, would it?"

Carly swallowed past the lump in her throat. "The sad thing is, I don't think Harvey knew who he was dealing with. Probably thought Bear Cove was like Mayberry. Didn't expect Bob to be a killer."

"Unfortunately, evil is everywhere."

She stepped out of the car. "Yes it is, but at least we have one less piece of the slime off the streets of our fair town." She led the way back inside. "Want some coffee?"

"That would be great."

Bradley came out of the kitchen and plopped onto the sofa. "Dad heard you guys coming and just put on another pot."

Carly and the police chief sat in the living room. He laid his head back on the sofa while she thought about everything that happened over the past few days. She straightened. "Of course, ducks in a row."

The chief opened his eyes. "Huh?"

"I talked to Joe yesterday, and he said Paulson was really excited about this story. But he couldn't tell him anything until he got all his ducks in a row. Seemed to think that was really funny, Joe said."

"And that applies how?"

"Bob is an amateur photographer who sells pictures of local sea birds. Ducks in a row."

"Oh. I thought it was an important clue."

She sighed. "It is. It confirms we were right about it being Bob."

He closed his eyes again. "That's good to know. I hate it when I arrest the wrong guy."

She chuckled. "Happened a lot back in Florida, did it?"

He opened one eye. "Is my coffee here yet?" Then he sat up straighter. "Only once. And that was one time too many."

Bradley returned and flopped into Mike's chair, then propped his head on his hand and sighed. "I just know I'm gonna fail my book report."

Carly crossed the room and sat beside him. "How come?"

"I still haven't found my stuff, and even if I did, I didn't see the eclipse. I don't have any pictures or anything. All the rest of my class will have cool stuff, but not me."

She ruffled his hair and pulled him close, inhaling the little-boy smell of him—all fresh outdoors, fabric softener, and no-tear shampoo. "First of all, we know where your bag is. Anita said it's in her shed. And secondly, just about nobody in all of Maine, outside Bear Cove, caught even a glimpse of the eclipse. It was too cloudy."

He lifted his head and looked at her, his eyes large and trusting. "Really?"

"Really." She kissed the tip of his nose. "And I don't think any of your classmates came here, did they?"

He wrinkled that nose, the freckles across his bridge resembling pebbles on a beach. "Nope." He smiled. "That's good news, right?"

"Right."

"So nobody will have nothing to write about?"

His father chuckled. "Anything."

Bradley nodded. "So I could make something up, and still get the best mark?"

Carly tapped his temple. "But if you think for a minute, you can come up with a great story that's true, one that nobody else but you could tell."

He squinted and pursed his lips then shook his head. "A true story?"

"Yes." She tapped his head again. "What happened to you that didn't happen to anybody else in your class? Or in town? Or maybe in the whole, wide world?"

He exhaled, shoulders slumped, then he brightened. "Nobody else was grabbed by a big, bad man and hidden in a shed. And I bet nobody else got to watch TV all day and eat junk food all the time." He closed his eyes and rubbed his tummy. "But I did get a tummy ache from too much sugar." He shook his head. "I won't do that again."

Carly pulled him into a close hug and covered his face with kisses. "No worries about that. Your parents won't let you out of their sight for a long time."

He pushed away. "How long?"

His father chuckled. "Until you're at least twenty-five!"

Bradley scrunched up his eyes and counted on his fingers. "That is a really long time."

$$$

As they said their good-nights later that evening and headed for their room, Carly touched Mike's arm. "Just about all the mysteries are solved."

"Just about?"

She opened the door and sat on the corner of their bed, patting the quilt beside her. "I think there's just one left."

Mike sat. "Only one? Can I have that in writing?"

She mock-punched his arm. "Can we be serious just for a minute?"

He nodded and forced the smile from his face, adopting his most stern look. "Serious. What mystery remains outstanding?"

"Are you going to tell me about the call from the doctor?"

His brow pulled down. "Doctor? You talked to all the doctors and nurses at the hospital."

She shook her head. "This wasn't about the accident. The doctor you talked to before that. Dr. Nick?"

"Were you eavesdropping on my call?"

"No. But you were in the hallway, and I was in the—wait a minute. You're trying to distract me from my question."

His mouth lifted in that endearing half-smile she loved so much. The one that proved he was teasing, yet a kind of apology at the same time for trying to pull one over on her. "Busted."

"So who is he? And why did you need to see him?"

Dread built like a wall of water behind a dam, threatening to burst through. If she lost Mike. . .

He exhaled. "First of all, let me set your mind at ease. It wasn't about me. It was about you."

"I don't need a doctor."

"It's just a nickname. I was trying to keep it a secret, but you won't leave it alone, will you?"

"A nickname? A secret? You must have hit your head harder than we thought in that accident because you aren't making a peck of sense. What are you talking about?"

The worry knot eased up a mite. Not much, but a little.

"I entered a contest that a radio station in Portland was running. And I won."

She clapped her hands. "Oh, how exciting. So are we going somewhere exotic?" She closed her eyes and rocked on the bed. "I hope it's got a beach. And sand. Maybe something with palm trees? And coconuts?" She opened her eyes. "Oh, did I ruin your surprise?"

"Not really. And no, it's not warm. Or exotic. Unless you consider downtown Portland in the spring warm. You won a day on a radio show as co-host of the oldies but goodies. You'll be on the Monday of the Memorial Day weekend." He grabbed her hands and pulled her to her feet, dancing her around the room before releasing her and collapsing to the bed beside her. "You know, like *Chantilly Lace* and *Nights in White Satin.*"

Oh, no. Coming in only slightly ahead of a root canal was the prospect of talking to people through a microphone for an entire day in a big city.

What was he thinking?

She gulped. "Maybe you should do it. You'd be a natural, with that great voice of yours. People always say you should have been a radio announcer."

He gripped her hands. "You hate it?" His shoulders slumped and his chin rested on his chest. "I thought you'd love it. And you'll have a few months to get used to the idea. The only thing is, it's the only day they can do it. Something to do with advertising rates or something. So they got approval from their parent company for that Monday. They figured folks would be listening to the radio as they travel and go around and do their errands and stuff, or while they're working around the house. I said we could do it because there wasn't anything booked that far out."

The phone on the bedside table rang. She glanced at it, then back to her husband. "Well, I—"

He sighed. "Go ahead. Answer it."

She did. "Hello?"

A woman's voice chuckled from the other end of the line. "Hi Carly, it's me. Gloria."

Carly glanced at her husband, who shrugged and headed for the bathroom. "Hi, Gloria. How are things?"

"Great. Listen, I know it's late, so I won't keep you long. Remember I promised you an Alaskan cruise? Well, that was a while back, and maybe you forgot. To thank you for getting me out of that jam I was in. Well, I didn't forget, so I went ahead and booked it. First one out of Seattle next cruise season. Sails on the Sunday of the Memorial Day weekend. So pack your bags—well, not yet, of course, but in a few months. You're going to Alaska."

"The Sunday of Memorial Day you said?"

"Yes. Hopefully you're not already booked, are you? Oh, please say you can go. I already booked a nice suite. And your airfare. You'll arrive the day before, stay in a hotel overnight. And I even booked you to stay a couple of extra days after you get back so you can sightsee around Seattle. It'll be the perfect little romantic getaway for you and Mike."

For once, Gloria was right.

It would be a perfect little romantic getaway for them.

One that *didn't* include a DJ in Portland.

Maybe she'd get some time to ponder the question of her faith— or lack of it.

"Thanks, Gloria. It's great."

She hung up, and headed for the bathroom. "Oh, Mike. . ."

Leeann Betts writes contemporary suspense, while her real-life persona, Donna Schlachter, pens historical suspense. She has released seven titles in her cozy mystery series, By the Numbers, with number 8, *A Deadly Dissolution*, releasing in June. In addition, Leeann has written a devotional for accountants, bookkeepers, and financial folk, *Counting the Days,* and with her real-life persona, Donna Schlachter, has published two books on writing, *Nuggets of Writing Gold* and *More Nuggets of Writing Gold,* a compilation of essays, articles, and exercises on the craft. She publishes a free quarterly newsletter that includes a book review and articles on writing and books of interest to readers and writers. You can subscribe at www.LeeannBetts.com or follow Leeann at www.AllBettsAreOff.wordpress.com All books are available on Amazon.com in digital and print, and at Smashwords.com in digital format.

Other Books By Leeann Betts:
Counting the Days: a 31-day devotional
In Search of Christmas Past – a novel
Available at Amazon.com in print & digital, & at Smashwords.com in digital

By the Numbers series featuring Carly Turnquist, forensic accountant
No Accounting for Murder
There Was a Crooked Man
Unbalanced
Five and Twenty Blackbirds
Broke, Busted, and Disgusted
Hidden Assets
Petty Cash
Available at Amazon.com in print & digital, & at Smashwords.com in digital

By Leeann and Donna:
Nuggets of Writing Gold — articles and essays on writing.
More Nuggets of Writing Gold – more articles & essays on writing
Available at Amazon.com in print & digital, & at Smashwords.com in digital

Books by Donna Schlachter:
Second Chances and Second Cups, A short story collection.
The Physics of Love: where the past, the present, and the future collide
The Mystery of Christmas Inn, Colorado
Christmas Under the Stars
Transformation – a devotional

Mended by God series
Broken Dreams, Mended Heart
Broken Dreams, Mended Family
Broken Dreams, Mended Marriage
Available at Amazon.com in print & digital, & at Smashwords.com in digital

From Barbour Publishing:
Echoes of the Heart — The Pony Express Romance Collection
A Prickly Affair — Bouquet of Brides Romance Collection
Train Ride to Heartbreak — Mail Order Brides Romance Collection
Detours of the Heart – MISSadventure Brides (releasing December 2018)

Follow us:
Donna: www.HiStoryThruTheAges.wordpress.com
Leeann: www.AllBettsAreOff.wordpress.com
We are also active on Facebook and Twitter
Sign up for our free quarterly newsletter and receive a free book:
Donna (historical) www.HiStoryThruTheAges.com
Leeann (contemporary) www.LeeannBetts.com